Nov

**Other Books by Durjoy Datta**

Of Course I Love You!
She Broke Up, I Didn't!
Ohh Yes, I Am Single!
You Were My Crush!
If It's Not Forever

# Now That You're Rich!

## . . . Let's Fall In Love!

Durjoy Datta
Maanvi Ahuja

GRAPEVINE INDIA

Grapevine India Publishers Pvt. Ltd.
Plot no.4, First Floor
Pandav Nagar,
Opposite Shadipur Metro Station,
Patel Nagar,
New Delhi - 110008
India
grapevineindiapublishers@gmail.com
contact@grapevineindia.in

First published by Grapevine India Publishers in 2011



Typeset and layout design: A & D. Co.



Printed and bounded in New Delhi

*To Shelly (1998-2009)*

*The bravest, cutest and smartest dog ever. We will miss you.*

# *Acknowledgements*

This acknowledgement wouldn't have been written if it were not for the people who read Of Course I Love You . . . Till I Find Someone better! and made us whatever we are today.

We thank all our readers. Thank you for everything. You guys rock ( . . . Only the ones who liked it)!

We thank quite a few people every time we write a book; no one really knows what they did to make us thank them. To be very honest, they didn't do anything.

But we would still like to thank hoards of people to make sure they buy themselves a copy.

We thank Sachin Garg, for last time we thanked him first . . . the book worked. Kanika Juneja, for everything the book is. And Naveen Kadyan, for being the awesome guy he is.

And the rest . . . for reasons that we have entirely made up on our own . . .

Neeti Rustagi for the discounts she promises me, Kanika Suri, Stuti Kapoor and boyfriend, Nishit Bhatnagar, Ekta Mehta for her sheer hotness, Mohit Gupta and girlfriend, Sachin Hans, Mukul Dalmiya, Namit Goel, Yogesh Kumar, Rishab Chhadda for his camera, Abhijit Bharat Kumar who hates what I write but still promotes it, Ankur Ashok for being the funniest guy ever, Narendra for his beer induced antics, Dishari Halder for her criticisms, Shubhangini Kaul, Mohit Mohnot for his wisecracks, Harish Singhania for nothing I can think of, Chhavi Khurana for inspiring a major character in the book, Abhishek Sachdev, Nitin Verma for being the inspiration on weight loss, the guys and girls we have had crushes on, my flatmate for being clean, all bloggers whether or not they visit ours, Sumit Sharma etc. etc.

We thank everybody at MDI, Gurgaon and everyone we

know at Hyderabad, hoping they would be moved by this mention.

We thank our families and Guruji for having high capacities of tolerance and love.

We thank our sisters, Rituparna and Tanvi separately because they wanted to see their name in print. Again.

For everything else, we thank ourselves.

# You Need To Hear This

I have always been terrible with secrets and stories that are never meant to be told or passed on. A very feminine trait, I know. But then, stories are meant to be told, aren't they?

Lazing in my cosy couch today, with a laptop in tow, I can't help but recall a story that I have told a million times, no matter how many times I have been asked to shut up.

But I find no reasons as to why I shouldn't pen this one down and entertain a few souls. And irritate a few others. But what the heck! I will still write it.

This one, I think, has all the elements:

a guy with a Porsche, a girl lost in love, selfish parents, loving siblings, a love scene on a thirteenth floor terrace, lecherous seniors, blackmail, life altering videos, hideous bosses, infinitely sexy co-workers, drunk guys professing undying love and last but not the least . . . Definitely not the least.

*Money.*

Fifty years after you get married you find women with black hair sexy. Women walking without a stick gorgeous. Whoever that woman might be, she won't be your wife.

Not that your wife would care as you eye another woman with your freshly treated-for-cataract eyes.

What she would care is whether she has to cry out hoarse for throat medicine or is there a nurse to take care of that.

Love makes the world go round. But money buys the tickets.

Maybe, love lasts a lifetime. Money lasts longer. *It pays for the funeral.*

Falling in love is easy. Choose the sweet guy who sits next to you in class, or the girl who does as much as to talk to you, exchange numbers, sweet and dirty messages alike through nights and days. And BAAM!

You are in Love.

So, what's wrong?

The analysis

Is the guy rich? Is the girl rich? Does the girl have a brother? What after thirty years? Will I be happy with a paunch where there had been washboard abs before? Will I be happy when they sag? Will I be happy to see her wrinkled smile twenty years down the line, with my daughter asking for a solitaire while taking birth control pills before eighteen? Will he be able to get me a ring and my son a bike at the same time?

One answer settles it all.

Marry rich, very rich.

We are all very nice people, and for us, relationships are meant to last a lifetime.

If they don't, the guy was a bastard. For the girls, she must be a slut.

So, till the time that changes, choose your date for tonight carefully. You might just end up spending a lifetime together.

Fall in love carefully. Wads of money usually break the fall. Often makes for a smooth landing.

So, now that the pearls of wisdom have trickled down my brains to the recesses of yours, let us go on with the story.

The four of them.

Overachievers. Geeks. Nerds. The people you would hate to be sitting in your examination hall with, the ones who ask for sheets after sheets while you look blankly at the question paper. Who would be out with the answer while you still look for your calculator figuring out which numbers to tap? Whom you would not consider as serious contenders while predicting class ranks. Olympiad winners. College gold medallist.

All four of them, brilliant minds.

The first amongst them, Abhi, exemplified everything I just said. He was an eighties virgin, yet to score it. The nineties were his sluts. He lusted for them.

He had led an uneventful life, the craziest thing he had ever done was to take an exam with a chapter not revised. So, let me start from the day he had spent his last day as a college topper, when something remotely *happening* happened.

# Abhi—Growing Up Troubles

It was the fourth of January and the air in the college campus was redolent with expectations and sweat of his fellow classmates who were still without a job.

There were more than a few pair of eyes on him; most of them had disgust dripping from them. A few greeted him. Others looked away. He had already been placed in a company which offered him seventeen lakhs per annum. He wanted more. This one was offering thirty. Three million a year.

He left the presentation and headed for the library where he came across few of his professors. They wished him luck and said they had full faith in his capabilities.

He had too, so did his fellow classmates. He was good enough to be hated.

*I need this. This is what I want to do.* He told himself and trudged to the library. He passed the college bookshop and spotted few of his classmates in an intense discussion with Raju bhaiya. Raju had seen hundreds of students spend the best three years of their lives in front of him. Years later, they would discuss him in their reunions. But Abhi would never be a part of those discussions. He had been too busy with books. Seniors. Professors' dicks. Sucking is a difficult job to do.

Macroeconomics, by Ravi Shastra. He flipped through the pages. There was nothing new. He flipped through some other books. Accounts. Business Studies. Law.

Same thing.

The last two years of spending hours, neck deep in those books, while others were looking down cleavages held him in good stead.

Abhi had been brought up in a single income family. His father worked in DDA while his mother was a housewife. The glaring difference between his father and his uncles' wealth always pinched him: their cars, their big houses, and the big rings on their fingers. He always felt he was missing out something. Though his parents did whatever they could for him, he did not like it when his uncle discussed business and laughed out at the losses that were more than his father's yearly income. He wanted to make it big. This was his day. His chance.

Abhi was always conspicuous by his presence. He was Delhi board topper, 2004, NTSE scholar and CA foundation rank one. Everybody knew who he was. Some girls even found him cute. Girls find even dogs cute. Big deal.

But I wouldn't really call him average looking with his just right complexion, lean frame and chocolate boy looks on a six foot frame. He was better looking than many guys around. But hiding everything behind huge rimmed glasses, dull shirts and oversized trousers wasn't the best thing to do. The white sport shoes under the dirt brown trousers just made things worse.

It had been hardly a few minutes that he had started reading an article on subprime losses and their fallout that he heard a meek squeaky voice of a girl.

Riya had just joined college and looked so. She stood no taller than Abhi's shoulder and had a baby face that had not left her since she was in eighth standard. She was *as* fair and as cute as they get. Beyond measure. Women have had a tendency to breast feed her, I have heard. Nice baby like eyes. Small pouty pink lips. The brightest shade of pink could be named after her. A big smile was her biggest asset, it never left her face.

She pulled up a chair and after congratulating him for his placement with HLL, the conversation shifted to other things.

'But all my friends are taking tuitions,' she said and her lips curved downwards when Abhi dismissed tuition centres.

'If you concentrate hard enough in classes and don't miss any, I don't think you need to spend so much on tuitions.'

'Yes, I guess. But you are a topper. It's easy for you to say this.'

'It's not that. Attend classes and you too will do well. It's easy.'

'But who will attend all the classes?' she asked and leaned back on her chair. A little shorter and her feet would not have touched the floor. 'There is so much to do. There is the choreography team, the western dance team . . . there are so many movies to watch . . . the new one . . . Johnny Depp is looking so hot in it, even though I don't like his beard . . . but that is okay . . . and there is this nice new party place near Vasant Kunj, you've got to go there . . . you just can't miss it. It is done in pink and blue . . . it is wonderful . . . and add to that, shopping and school friends . . . there is no time left . . . Oh! And there is new Bercos in Kamla Nagar and it is so *eww* . . . but there is this small shop near it which has these real nice earrings . . .'

She went on for *long*. Abhi did not mind, he was busy noticing her. Her white T-shirt hung down from a shoulder and showed a strap—pink.

Her T-shirt spelled out—*Sugar,* in pink. There was *perfect* colour harmony. Earrings and shoes. Shoes and bangles. Bangles and hair colour. There were some twenty shades of pink on her that day. She even smelled pink.

'Riya?' somebody shouted from behind them.

'Oh . . . I must get going. We are going for a movie today. Thank you, sir.'

'Missing classes?'

'Yes,' she crinkled her nose and smiled. 'Bye,' she said, clutched her bright pink handbag and left.

He followed the skin fit jeans with little fake diamonds on them and the screaming pink handbag as she hopped across the library and joined her friends. For a girl of her height, she had considerable curves. A miniature Beyoncé. Add a few inches, make her a decade older and she would look like a porn star. But, somebody up there wanted her to look like a kid.

Abhi smiled at himself and got back to his newspaper, running the conversation over and over again in his mind, reliving it again. Blood had rushed from every vein to his face and his cheeks had turned into a shade of red.

This was the defining day of his life.

He had the longest conversation with a girl, ever.

And he was through.

Silverman Finance.

Geeks fall in love. Way too quickly. For the simple reason that it is not every day that a girl so cute comes up to them and starts a conversation.

Abhi was in *love*. Deep true love!

It was his third *Maggi* and his stomach revolted but he could not think of a better reason to sit outside her class which faced the canteen.

The hour changed. The class changed . . . But there was no sign of her.

The last three days of wait finally yielded as she walked past him, surrounded by friends, hopping between them, screeching at the top of her voice as she begged them to miss another class. Abhi sat up and prayed that she would notice him.

She and another classmate of hers stayed back. The others entered the class.

Abhi alternated between staring at his plate and looking at her, keeping a page half turned to look busy. She was in the same colours as she was that day. She wore a pink tube with a shrug over it. Her navel showed, and normally it would look sluttish and sexy . . . but on her . . . it looked just cute! The sun reflected off her face and it glowed. Bright yellow. Her straight pressed hair that came down to her waist shone. She did not see him.

He sat there, waiting for her to notice him, often changing positions, getting up and then sitting down again, rustling the pages in order to catch her attention. *Nothing* worked.

Finally, he got up to leave.

Just as he crossed her, she noticed him and came running to him, her handbag, a different one, but pink still, waving in the air.

'Hi! Where are you going?' she asked. 'Oh . . . by the way, congratulations for getting through! I told all my friends about you . . . and they went nuts that I know the guy who got the best placement! But then I told them that we have just talked once and then they were like okay . . . but you've got to admit . . . I am your lucky charm. We talked and you got through

. . . so I deserve a treat . . . I know this place . . . really nice . . . and you look so tired . . . what happened?'

Abhi had gone red in the face again.

'Nothing.'

'Okay . . . listen . . . I got to go now . . . I have this practice . . . the western dance thing . . . it is in two months . . . you have got to see it . . . okay . . . got to go . . . bye!'

'Okay . . . bye.'

She left him smiling ear to ear.

Gradually, she started noticing him around all the time. Ignoring a fly buzzing in your face is usually quite tough. Small conversations brewed. Numbers were exchanged. The day that happened, Abhi spent hours staring at it. Free time between classes was spent at the CCD nearby. Messages were exchanged, day in, day out. Generally, if you are exchanging more than twenty messages with a girl in a day, I would say you are in *love*.

They were getting closer each passing day. Her innocent charm had him in knots every time she smiled at him. His brains helped her do whatever she could not manage herself in days.

'I really don't need this,' Abhi said to her as she held out a pair of jeans to him faded on the oddest of places. She had taken him to accompany her on one of her shopping sprees, but seeing him in the mirror, so awfully dressed, she couldn't help herself.

'Are you crazy? This is what everyone is wearing these days . . . Seen OC? 90201? Everyone . . . you just *got to* have one of these. Trust me, they will look awesome. You have the face and the physique for it. Just go, try them . . . next, we will try those ones there . . . they are a little expensive but you can't miss out on those . . .' She said as she pushed him into the fitting room.

She got him two new pair of jeans, some T-shirts and rimless spectacles . . . and I hate to say this, but he looked good. She stood next to him, clutching his arm, as he stood in front of the mirror. A red T-shirt with an illegible graphic on it, a clinging pair of jeans and new spectacles, Abhi could hardly recognize himself. Riya kept pulling his jeans down, every time he tried to pull it up to his navel.

He admitted that it was the best he had ever looked.

There was not a time in the day when he wasn't thinking about her. Her face never left his eyes . . . her voice, his ears. He spent hours sitting and staring at blank walls, running their conversations through his head and recounting times they had spent together. The messages were read over and over again. He had lost consciousness of time and space. He was with her, every moment, every second of the day. He never felt so good in his life. He felt nice about himself. Loved. Her face was the most beautiful thing in the world for him. Those eyes, those lips, that smile.

Months passed and their friendship grew stronger. Abhi was the first person who was told everything: Screwed class tests, a bitching friend, new shoes at Puma, stringy tops at Kazo. Everything.

First love is always tricky. It promises much. More often than not, it is just a practice ground for subsequent relationships. To Abhi, it did a world of good. He had changed from a nerd to a college hottie in a matter of days. Cool tees, *chappals,* random accessories et al. His oiled hair now got a rough grunge cut falling over his eyebrows. And finally, his tongue didn't end up in knots while talking to a girl. He was a different guy now. Riya's company was doing wonders to him.

All what was going on, left Abhi with no doubt that she was as much in love with him as he was with her. I do not blame him for this. He was too stupid to see anything, too stupid to see Riya walking away from him whenever her phone beeped. Too stupid to see her smiling stupidly when a message came. Riya never felt the need to tell him about Arjun. Girls usually never do. But, Guys are expected to understand. But, guys never do.

What are you doing tonight? *Does she want to have sex with me?*

Do you live alone? *She wants to come over?*

Do you have a girlfriend? *She wants to be mine?*

What girls mean by these sentences I would never know. Neither did Abhi. I usually assumed the latter.

However, all that he used to think got smashed that day at the choreography competition, which Riya was participating in. She had handed over her cell phone to Abhi just before she went backstage. It started ringing after a while.

*Sweetheart calling . . .*

Abhi's mind went blank for a few seconds. He dismissed it thinking it must be a female friend of hers.

The call was not answered.

Six calls were not answered.

Abhi with trembling hands looked at the number. Only the last digit was different from Riya's. He had *heard* of many couples who buy those numbers. Cheap calling rates. They talk throughout the night. The guy/girl gets bored. They fight.

They break up. Same story everywhere.

Money keeps a relationship going. Go in for the most expensive call plan. Call less, talk less. Keep the mystery alive. Let it be a year before you know your girl has a dog.

He checked the inbox as Riya came on stage.

Every second message was from the same number.

*Hi. Where are you? Miss you. See you soon.*

*Best of luck, sweetheart. Might get a little late. Sorry. Love. Muah.*

*I love you. You are the best thing that ever happened to me. Lots of slurpies. Muah.*

Abhi looked at her dancing and noticed a distant, indifferent look in her eyes. He re-read the messages and checked the call details. He was crushed. He resisted the urge to throw the phone away. Abhi looked for somebody of her batch and handed over her things to him, trying to keep back the tears.

He wanted to leave that very moment but waited till the end of her performance.

He waited till she came out, still looking for somebody. The very next second a smart, nice looking guy appeared and hugged her. The embrace was more than just a friendly hug and tears rolled down Abhi's cheeks.

Abhi spent the next two hours walking around aimlessly on the streets of Delhi University living every moment again. He checked the call timings of every single call and read every single message. He read the tissue paper she had once given him after writing something on it and threw it away. Only to pick it again, un-crumple it and keep it safe. He could still see her smiling right in front of him. He realized he had not asked her to love him. It wasn't her fault. It wasn't his fault. He wiped his tears and slowly walked back home. Smiling, as he saw her smiling. Right in front of him.

He messaged her.

*Your performance was great.*

After a few days of taking care to be out of sight of Riya, she caught hold of him while he was entering the class.

'Abhi?' she called out.

He looked back to see her running towards him. He had been dying to see her.

'Yes.'

'Can we talk . . . Unless you have something to do? Please . . . I have something to tell . . . why did you leave that day? Can we . . . Café Coffee Day has this new fat free coffee and it is fabulous . . . we just *have to* go . . .'

'I have a class.'

'Miss it . . . I have so much to talk to you . . .'

'No, I can't.'

Abhi snubbed her and entered the class.

After a few minutes of macro-economics, he walked out of the class and ran in the direction where Riya had gone.

She was sitting on the pavement, polishing her nails, but the glint in her eyes was missing.

'Hey . . .'

'Missing it?'

'Yeah.'

'You can attend it if you want to . . . but the coffee is real nice . . . but let this dry out first . . . This is a new one . . . my mom's friend got it from The States . . . it's teak pink . . . real nice, no?'

'You wanted to talk about something,' Abhi said irritably.

'Yes, are you pissed at me? You don't pick up my calls and don't even reply to my messages. And you went that day without even meeting me . . . I should be the one pissed at you . . .'

'Is this what you wanted to talk about?' he asked. His heart was aching to say that he loved her.

'No . . . yeah . . . It's about Arjun . . . That guy . . . doesn't even know how to eat with a fork and he makes me wait . . . and that day . . . he wore a green check shirt . . . that too in front of my friends . . . who wears that? I mean . . . he is so tacky . . .'

'What is your point, Riya?'

'He stood me up . . .'

'So . . . that can happen.'

'Are you kidding me? I was there standing in the heat for two hours . . . I was out of sunscreen and he didn't come . . . he had his phone switched off . . .' Riya, for the first time, stopped talking without interruption. She had tears in her eyes.

'What happened?' Abhi said, now paying attention.

'It is just that . . . I think he doesn't love me anymore . . . It is been so long since he ever got me something nice . . . we don't meet that often anymore . . . I mean . . . I cancelled my shopping date for a date with him and he simply doesn't care . . . He just cares about his friends . . . and that friend of his . . . the one who I told you about . . . *arey* . . . the girl who wears tacky platform heels . . .' The tears had started peeking out. 'I love him Abhi . . . I don't know what is happening to him . . .'

'Everything will be fine,' Abhi said half-heartedly.

'I hope so . . . and I hope he stops wearing those cargos he bought like a year ago . . .' The tears were still trickling down.

Just as Abhi was about to keep his hand on her head, he saw

the familiar face walking in their direction.

'I think your boyfriend is coming.'

She looked up and immediately started wiping off her tears. She took out a handkerchief and rubbed it all across her face trying to remove all remnants of her tears.

'Do I look okay?'

'Yes.'

'Are my eyes red?'

'A little bit.'

'Does it look like I was crying?'

'Not really.'

'The mascara?'

'Looks fine.'

'The cheeks?'

'Pink.'

'We are . . .'

'Best friends,' Abhi said. Riya had taught him this.

Abhi watched them leave, with Arjun trying to put an arm across and keep her close.

Abhi now recalled it. Arjun used to drop her to college sometimes. He had a big car, Honda or something. Not that he was very good-looking, but everything he wore was expensive. Somewhere deep inside, he felt he wasn't worth Riya. He wasn't as swanky as Arjun was. It had started pinching him. More than his uncles' immense wealth, it was Arjun's affluence that bothered him.

Arjun's behaviour towards Riya had been deteriorating by the day and she had been living in denial. Double denial. She knew she was being wronged. And she *knew* she was refusing to see it.

Riya's complaints about him had gone beyond mere missed dates, bad shoes and stinking armpits. Their relationship was seeing real troubles now. Arjun had changed his relationship status to *single* on Facebook and was entertaining random girls. One question asked and Riya was shouted at for being nagging. It happened every day. The time she spent crying increased.

Getting close to Riya had been two edged for Abhi. For every time she said she never had a friend like him, he felt privileged. Every time he chose a nail polish for her, he felt important. Every time he was the first person to see the new streaks in her hair, he felt complete.

However, seeing her so madly in love with someone else killed him. He wished her perfectly manicured hands were in his, not Arjun's.

Riya had noticed Abhi's changed behaviour but she chose to ignore it. Crushes are hard to deal with. A crush problem is harder than a lust problem. A boob peek doesn't solve it. Nothing does. Everyone insists things wouldn't change, but they do.

'Will you please stop crying?' Abhi said for the seventh time that evening. Arjun was still being a real jackass and it took a toll on Riya.

Riya's condition had gone from bad to worse. She had started talking less. And that day was the first time he had seen her without her eye makeup. Not that she looked any less cute.

'Sorry.'

'You don't have to be.'

It was the same story every time. Arjun did something that she didn't think was right and she spent time crying over it in front of Abhi till the time she ran out of tears and simply forgot what she was crying about.

'What happened?' . . .

'Nothing.'

'I want to know. I can't see you like this. So quiet. You haven't even shopped for a week now. No new shoes. No bangles. Even your earrings don't match your shoes today . . . .'

'Really . . .?' She checked out her shoes and smiled behind those tears. 'Of course . . . they do match . . . You are so mean'

'So . . . now tell me . . .'

'He says I am boring.'

'As in?'

'As in, *physically.*' She kept crying. 'He is asking me to give in . . . Sleep with him . . .'

'*Is he insane?* What the . . . . How can he ask you to do that . . .?'

'He says every friend of his is doing it and he expects me . . .'

'What did you do?'

'No . . . I can't . . . I love him . . . despite everything, he is sweet . . .'

'So . . . what will you do?'

'I don't know. Maybe he is right. Even Kritika has done it with her boyfriend. So . . . but . . .'

'*So?*'

Every word of hers hit him like a boulder thrown right at his face. He knew in all probability that Riya was physically involved with Arjun but hearing it from her mouth made him bleed. And that she would do it because he wanted it, filled him with unbridled rage.

The girl he loved so much. The girl he could give all for.

He couldn't stop his tears.

'Leave him,' he said and wiped his tears off.

'I can't.'

'What do you mean *you can't*? Of course you can! You are cute . . . and smart . . . you can . . .'

'I can't . . . I love him . . . I love him so much . . . Just last week, he got me this real cute teddy bear key chain . . . and then we even went to that place . . . Oh . . . no . . . that was you! Sorry . . . but I love him . . . I always will . . .'

'*You call this love*? Haan? You call this love? He is bloody abusing you. Can't you see that?' Abhi's voice started to rise.

'But . . .'

'What but . . . that bastard . . . all he wants is to fuck you . . . Are you really this blind . . .' He stood up and started moving around in circles coming close to her and shouting at her.

'Abhi . . . mind your language . . . he is my . . . and it's none of your business . . .'

'Mind your own business? What the hell? You know what my business is? I will show you . . . no wait I will show you what my business is.' He rummaged through his bag throwing half his things around and took out three neatly done assignments.

'This is my business. This is economics.' He threw it in her lap. 'Microeconomics. And law. Last date tomorrow. You don't even know when these were given. Who did this? *I did.* All night. I did it. Not that bastard. I love you. I am the one who has been in love with you for the last six months. Not him. I am the one who is listening to you and seeing you cry every day. Not him. And what do you do?' He threw his hands in the air. 'You sleep with him. *Perfect.*'

'Abhi! One word and I will slap you.'

'What one word? Go say that to him. Why? What happened? You can say anything to me, but not to him. He is the one who brought you to this level. He is the one who treats you like shit. He goes out with other girls and you don't say a thing to him . . . he doesn't love you . . . I do. He doesn't . . .'

'Enough. I am leaving,' she said as she gathered her bag, wiped her tears off and turned to leave.

'Yes . . . Go . . . go to him . . . sleep with him . . . I don't care about you . . . go away . . . Go sleep with the whole college, I don't care! Don't know how you came here? I hope you fail exams . . . you anyway will . . .'

'What?' She turned back. 'Abhi, just because you have some big placement doesn't mean we all are nothing . . . and what are you? You were nothing when I met you . . . nobody would have done as much as look at you . . . you nerd . . . I made you what you are . . . I did . . . otherwise you would have been still roaming around the college alone . . . eating Maggi . . . .'

'At least I don't sleep with everyone like a slut . . .'

'What?' At this, she hit him with her handbag repeatedly, while breaking into tears and howling aloud.

Abhi stood there realizing what he had just done and slumped on the pavement, with tears in his eyes as Riya walked away from him.

Crushes on friends are always disastrous. So was this one.

After that incident, Abhi just wanted to get through the remaining few days left in college as quickly as possible. He tried to date a few girls in between, but nothing great happened. The good part was that they were those who did not match up to his expectations and not the other way round. This was new for him.

He dreamt of the days when he would earn more than ten of his classmates put together and girls would drool over him; girls as good as Riya was, cute. *Pink.*

Silverman meant new opportunities for Abhi. But for Shruti, it meant a new life, away from hers. It pains me to think of the life Shruti led before Silverman happened to her. If I were sensitive to a dying duck in my arms, I might even have shed a tear or two. So, before I take out the tissues, let us go to the day she had another sad day in another sad month in another sad year of her sad life.

# Shruti's Mind Said. *Run.*

She wiped the sweat from her brow. Jagjit's face flashed before her eyes as she entered the room. Her hair was neatly tied in a ponytail behind her back and she had dressed up in a crisp white shirt and slim trousers. With pouted lips, as if done intentionally, gorgeous legs and a stomach so flat that it would put a road roller to shame Shruti could easily have been mistaken for an exotic Indian model on those four inch pumps she wore. Not to forget the sharp features and a sharp nose and eyes to go with it. She got nothing from her parents, both fat and ugly looking. Maybe her complexion and I would thank them for it. The thought of dark chocolate sweet smelling skin still makes my hair stand on end. Shruti used to be one of the most sought after girls in college. Her cotton fitted shirts that clung to her body and showed what she wore inside and the knee length skirts were the talking point for every guy with testosterone, in college. Nobody could fathom how she fell for Sachin, the college stationery shopkeeper's son.

'Good morning, Shruti.'

'Good morning.' Her voice cracked.

'You want to drink something before we start.'

She nodded, picked up the glass and emptied it.

'Why finance, Shruti?'

'I have always been interested in this field sir. I have done CFA level one and CA foundation level. I have also done my internship at Morgan Stanley and Barclays. It is in the file. Everything. The college certificates too. I also won the business quiz at DCE. I won the Business plan contest and the singing competition and the math quiz and the entrepreneurship seminar . . .' she said and opened the file and thrust the certificates out in front of him. She was panicking.

'I don't need to see those. Why Silverman?'

'Sir, it is because . . . it is the best financial institution in the world and I really want to work there,' she said this and her mind drew a blank. She just sat there, rubbing her hands and looked down at them.

'And . . . ?'

'Sir . . . that is the reason. I really want to work at Silverman.'

'Or is it the money?'

She stared blankly at him. Her head spun like she was in a revolving chair.

'Yes,' she said. 'Just the money?'

'No sir.'

'Then?'

'Yes sir. Sorry sir. But I am ready to work hard,' she said, her voice failing her and her head started spinning again. 'Sir, I have scored well and I will do well there too. I promise. Just give me a chance and I assure you, I will do well. Sir, I promise. I worked hard all my life and will continue doing so.' She was almost begging.

'Calm down, Shruti.'

She nodded furiously as she felt it slipping through her fingers.

A few questions came about balance sheets and accounts and she breezed through them. The interviewer made sure that her out of the ordinary marks were not a sustained fluke, and she was a brilliant kid as her marks suggested. Studies, exams, college rankings were the only things that she cared for in her god forsaken life. She had made sure that *that* part of her life was perfect.

She walked all the way home that day. The walk back to her place meant a lot to her. It had changed her life. Had her father not seen Sachin put his hand across her on the way back home one day, she wouldn't be getting married this year. The walk didn't really decide what would happen to her, but it brought her fate closer than it was.

'What took you so long?' her mother asked as soon as she stepped into her house.

'The interview went on very long,' she said as she made her way to her room.

'It is eight. Do you think we are fools? Where were you?' she asked as she grabbed hold of her hand.

'I was in college.'

'Then why didn't you pick up your phone?'

'I was in the interview.'

'All the time?' she asked. 'I will not tell your father this time but the next time you are late I will tell him, and then you face him.'

'Whatever,' she shrugged off, went into her room and threw her bag on the bed. Her mother followed her. Shruti did not have a room till she was eighteen. She used to share one with her brother. After a month of discussion, the store room was cleaned up and she was shifted there. Despite earnest requests from her brother, that he wanted to take that damp, dark, squalid miniscule room. Her brother had his tenth boards that year. Shruti was slapped for persuading her brother to ask for the store room.

'Next time you talk to me like that, I will throw you out of this house. Then go into Sachin's arms and do whatever you want to. Ever since you have met him you have forgotten all about us. That lowly bastard . . .'

'Mom.'

'Shut up, Shruti. And keep your tone down. You are such a selfish daughter. You have no responsibility towards the house. Look at your room. Don't you have eyes? Have you ever bothered to clean it? We don't have twenty servants here to do the job. I have to do it. You don't realize how much you take us for granted. No matter how much freedom we give you, you still want more. And what do you give us? Your grandmother has been coughing for the last three days, have you bothered to ask her how she's feeling? All you want is your college, your job, your career, your friends. This is the last time I am telling you Shruti, forget about the job and dare you say a word about that in front of your father or Guptaji. It is your luck that you are getting such a big man to marry you.'

'He is a divorcee.'

She got slapped. And again. Her mother's shrieks filled up the room.

'So what? That girl was a witch. She didn't know how to cook. Even took up a job. What do you expect? A wife of such a rich man to work? They have done a lot for your father and for whatever we have done for you, you have to keep him happy. It will be shameful if you do anything inappropriate there. But what do you care? All you think about is yourself. Even if we die, I don't think you will shed a single tear. Why don't you kill us yourself than putting us through all this?'

Moms are quite brilliant at this. I do not know where they

get it from, but they have this innate capability. You spill milk today and you will be shouted at, for not scoring well in math exam that you took five years ago and thereby spoiling the family name.

'But . . . I have done nothing to get him. I don't deserve him.'

'Shruti!' her mother shouted and slapped her again. She started howling and crying. 'Dare you answer back to me. They can take away this house. It is on their mortgage. You know we are neck deep in debt, don't you? How can you be so insensitive? My own daughter? How can you? I wish you had died at birth. At least I wouldn't have to see this day.'

She kept sobbing, a little softly now. It always worked. Shruti felt a tinge of guilt in her heart.

'I will do what you say,' she mumbled.

'No, do whatever you want. Kill us. That is what you want, do it. I am ashamed to have a daughter like you. Don't talk to me. Go and make *rotis* now,' she said and left the room as the bell rung. It was Shruti's father.

Shruti started making *rotis* and overheard the conversation between her parents which was deliberately loud enough just to make her hear what they were talking.

'I am sure she will blacken our faces some day. And that is after everything we do for her. I always knew one day she will turn her back to us,' her father bellowed. 'I am sure she was with that bastard. She is so brainless to not think of Jagjit. He likes her so much and she is such a waste. Call her.'

Her mother called her loudly.

'Yes,' she said tremblingly. She wished her brother was around. She wouldn't get hit then.

'Shruti, this is going too far. Just because we have given you freedom doesn't mean you will exploit it. I don't want to know why you were so late today but have decided something and you will have to do it. No college from tomorrow. You will go to Jagjit's place and talk to his mother. It has been three months since we promised to get the two of you married and they have not seen your face up till now. What impression do you think you are leaving on them? I do not want to hear any excuse. You have studied enough. Nothing will come out of it. Anyway once you get married you are going to sit at home and serve him.'

'But Papa . . . the marriage is a year away . . .'

'Don't you dare answer back. You will do what I ask you to do. You get that? Go to your room.'

'But I want to do this job till the time I get married.'

'We are not discussing it,' her father said as he sipped his whisky. He was a big, fat, balding old man, who in his youth had stood tall as a light pole and strong as a boulder. His word was the rule. People feared him. But then, times change, a few business deals went awry, he lost his confidence, even his name in the business. That was when Jagjit's father lent him money for a business that failed, spiralling him into debt worth crores and alcoholism. For now, the only place he was still feared was in his daughter's heart. His hand was heavy and she knew that.

'Why not? I want to do it.'

'Why? You are not going to do it all your life. Help your mother till the time you get married. Help her out. She is getting old and you still suck her blood. Look at her. Don't you feel pity, growing fat and roaming around with boys while she works in the kitchen all day?'

'I thought it would help in the dowry.'

Her father looked at her in sheer disbelief. 'What? A two paisa job and you will pay for your dowry?' he said mockingly.

'It is 2.5 lakhs per month.'

'What?' her parents echoed. Her father gulped down the whisky.

'Show me the offer letter,' her mother said.

'We will get it tomorrow,' she said.

'Then we will talk about it tomorrow.'

She walked to her room, closed the door behind her and pinned her ears to the door and listened to what her parents had to say.

Their tongues had started wagging. They were now hatching plans of how they would lie to the Gupta family about her doing a job. They would tell them that she is at her maternal grandmother's place. She closed her eyes and wished she could run away.

Hyderabad.

She prayed.

The next day, with her hands lathered with detergent she picked up the phone. It was from the placement cell.

She was through.

Everything seemed to change around her. Her eyes, always sunken, now had a twinkle in them. Her walk had a spring in it.

The only thing that did not change was her brother's love for her.

'Run away,' he said.

'What are you saying?'

'Run away,' he said again as he closed his book. It was his board exams that year. Cable connections had been cut.

Computer wires had been taken apart. Shruti's protests that these were not done when she took her board exams were looked down upon with scorn. She was slapped and told how selfish she was.

'I am serious, *Didi*. They will get you married here and you know that.'

'Yes. But there is nothing I can do,' she said as her mind raced with possibilities.

'Yes. You can. I am sure they will let you go to Hyderabad. They want the money and you know that. But you don't have to go through it. Once you settle there and have a few months behind you, stop sending them money and refuse to come back. That is it,' he said. It was a brave thing for him to say at his age.

'It is not possible. You wouldn't understand.'

'I do. Mom and dad will never talk to you. Dad will run into trouble with Gupta ji with loans to pay. But what has that got to do with *you*? You can't push yourself into this because our alcoholic father and overspending mother led themselves into this. Didi, the day I get in to an engineering college, I will forget I ever had them.'

'What are you saying, Archit? They love you.'

'They do? I don't think so. And even if they do, it is because I am their son. Once I get a job, I will help the family. And the day I get the job, they will marry me off and torture the girl to death for money. I am not going to be part of all that.'

It was almost as if the two of them had switched ages.

'Don't say that. They have brought us up and . . . '

'So what, *Didi*? Every parent does that. They have done nothing special. You were pushed inside the kitchen when you were six and mother spent all her time watching television. What special thing did they do? Dad could spend on his whisky while I had to wait months for a new bag. I got it eventually, but had it been you, you wouldn't have seen it ever. Just because they fed us for all these years doesn't give them any right to govern us. I am tired of all this.'

'Hmm . . . but what if . . . I lose the job someday and then . . . ?'

'You will not, Didi. You know you are good. And even if you do, you will find another one. And in any case, I will start earning in a few years. There is nothing that can go wrong here.' He smiled at this.

'What? Why are you smiling?'

'Didi . . . You are beautiful. Even if you don't find a job, you will find someone worthy enough of you, someone rich, very rich. Grab him. Things will be just fine,' he said and started laughing.

'Shut up.'

'Why? You still love Sachin?' he asked and the corner of her eyes filled up. Sachin was the son of the stationary shop owner at her college. Somehow, both of them struck a friendship and fell in love. After her father saw them and Sachin saw the bruise marks on Shruti's face the next day, he stopped coming to the shop, and Shruti never saw him again. They were a strange pair.

'I don't,' she said as she wiped off her tears. Some relationships are strange. They hardly talk. They hardly meet. They look into each other's eyes and spend a lifetime.

Just then, their parents entered the room and the conversation stalled.

Shruti had made no efforts to trace him and neither had he.

Three months hence, she was standing at the airport, her parents struggling to find words to bid her good bye. While she was issued warnings about staying away from boys and what would happen if she didn't, she was also hugged and they said that they really cared for her. Her parents knew this was a gamble, sending her to a different city, with no supervision and lots of money. But they had taken months to decide that they would let her go. They had made their calculations and it fitted right with their plans. It was worth the risk. And the money.

She disappeared behind the clearance gates, looking back once at her brother who smiled and winked at her.

*Run,* her mind said.

So while Shruti had been counting days for the day she would leave that place, and time hardly seemed to pass, for Saurav time was running out . . . quick.

Still a virgin, his school friends studying engineering abroad were doing it as frequently as he changed clothes . . . and he wasn't feeling any good about it.

One of the few things that you lose, or you don't, when you are in IIT: your virginity.

# Saurav— Lose It Before You Lose College

How many times has it happened that you look at a rich kid getting down from a big car and wished you were him or her? What would you do if you were him or her?

One thing you would NOT do is—Study. Study till you lose your balls.

But what if no matter what you do, may it be staring down at your teacher's cleavage as she bends or staring up your classmate's skirt, whatever the teacher says in class sticks in your ears, moves down from the veins and remains in your body till you puke it out during an exam.

If that happens to you, you are either an IITian or going to be one: a place without any cleavages and skirts. So, there you study. And top your exams.

To cut it short, you are Saurav: enviably rich; enviably brainy; enviably nerdy.

Saurav had been born with a silver spoon in his mouth. He was the new generation - educated rich. Life was an extended dream for him. He never wanted anything from life, life just happened to him.

It was unfair to the world when he got through Silverman

Finance. But all these things were one of the small things that happened to him.

He had bigger issues at hand.

Freud once said, *if you don't lose your virginity before twenty four, you will always be a loser*. Or something like that.

His friends from school had warned him about it when he cleared his entrance examinations for IIT, but he didn't pay heed.

Samrat. Kapoor. Kiran. All his guy friends had done it within the first few months that they landed in Holland, the US and the UK respectively. He was still a virgin.

They took out time to send him pictures of themselves in parties with beer glasses in hands and half naked women in their arms. While all he did was sending them scanned copies of his nine-point something IIT mark-sheets. They all had almost the same future ahead of them. Just that while they fucked, he got fucked!

'I am just waiting for the right time . . . I can't sleep with just anybody . . .' Saurav said unconvincingly.

'You are a *guy*! We can sleep with anybody with breasts . . . Just go find a girl!'

'But it would be the first time. I want it to be special. I can't just . . .'

'Don't give me that crap, man. Every time that dick of yours goes into something wet, you will feel special, trust me! Just go ahead . . . and stop fooling yourself with the virginity bullshit . . . It is not the 1800s.'

'It is not so easy here . . . And I am not the smartest around here . . . you know that . . .'

'I do, man . . . but there must be one girl . . . at least one in the whole of Delhi . . . who can think about sleeping with you, dude! You just have to find her . . . She won't come to you. And you are a rich guy, man! You drive your own Audi . . . IIT and stuff! Girls love all that . . . trust me . . .'

'But where . . .'

'Anywhere! Join cooking classes if you have to . . . lay an auntie . . . I don't fucking care . . . But do something . . .'

'I will try.'

They hung up. His inferiority complex touched new heights every time he talked to his friends.

Saurav was five ten and looked shorter. He was girlishly fair. He weighed a staggering one hundred and twenty kilos and looked more. It had been years that he had seen his toes. Fat defined him.

As soon as he got through Silverman Finance, he joined a slew of classes to find a girl who would look through those layers of fat and see his pure, love craving heart within. Maybe even his dick. Or at least get clicked pecking him. Or hugging him. Anything!

Guitar classes. No success. There were too many guys smarter, sexier and thinner.

Dance classes. He registered but when the latex covered dance instructor bent down and showed her little valley, the girls watched him lick his lips in the mirror and he blew his chance. Not that he had any.

Gym. Finally he was among his own breed. Fat, flabby bodies sweating on treadmills. Working out on bench-presses. Men and women alike.

He looked at her. She was on a treadmill stacking up miles and was too big to be missed. Pun intended. She was fat. Some would call her cute. Fat round face, slit eyes and almost as fair as anyone could realistically get.

'Hi,' Saurav said and tried hard not to pant while walking on the lowest speed on the treadmill.

The girl looked at him, smiled and kept walking. After a while she stepped down from the treadmill, walked up to the nearest couch and flopped on it.

Saurav followed her.

'Hi.'

'Do I know you?' The girl said wiping her face with a towel.

'Umm . . . no. But we can know each other.'

'Excuse me?'

'I mean, I have been noticing you for a few days and I think you are incredibly cute.'

'That is because I am too fat to look smart or sexy.'

'I beg to differ.'

'Isn't this your first day here?'

'So, have you been noticing me, huh?' he said, trying to sound sexy. It certainly didn't work. A fat man can't talk like James Bond and get away with it. I say it from experience.

'Obviously. You are the fattest around here. I felt good when you walked in.'

'Okay.'

'Don't worry. A few months and you will be as thin as me!' she laughed. Saurav found that cute.

'I hope so.' More than actually laying her, he was imagining how their wedding photographs might look like.

'Hmm . . . ' She took out a water bottle and took a sip.

'Can we go out sometime? Like coffee or anything . . .? If you don't mind?' he asked, his fingers crossed.

'I do mind. But then, I have nothing else to do after this. So how about now?'

'Perfect.'

They both changed into their regular clothes and moved

out of the gym. While Saurav had hidden everything under the triple XL track suit that he was wearing, Megha was bursting out of her jeans and T-shirt. Saurav, nonetheless, found her great. Even sexy, he told me.

Yes, at twenty two, it was his first date. Not that Saurav was shy, but the very fact that it seemed like he was pregnant with triplets killed his chance with any girl. And IIT hardly gave him any breathing space for that matter.

'What do you do?' she asked him.

'I am studying. IIT Delhi. B. Tech,' he said.

'What? Are you kidding me?' she exclaimed.

'No, I am not,' he said and fished out his ID.

'I don't need that. But seriously? IIT? You don't look like that. I mean I don't want to offend you, but you look like a property dealer's son or something.'

'Why do you say that?'

'You know. Fat, this huge a car and everything, and flirting with me . . . '

'When did I flirt with you?'

'You did.'

'I didn't.'

'Whatever.'

'So, where are we going?' Saurav asked. He was really counting on his chances now.

'You tell me. You asked me out.'

Samrat's words echoed in his ears and he did the unthinkable.

'My place,' he said in a very low tone hoping the honk of the car would drown it out. *I was kidding*, he would say that if she were to make a face on that, he had decided.

'Cool. Let's go,' she said.

Saurav blew his circuit right then. The near impossible just happened. He started thinking about what all reasons could be there for a girl to come to his place. Was he cute? Was she lusty? Did it even mean anything? Was he thinking too much? Was the gymming working?

He parked the car in the driveway and walked past the wide-eyed guard who was yet unaware of his master's new ways.

They went up to his room and cleared his bed of the laptop and his strewn books and asked her to sit.

'Can you switch off the light?' she asked him. His head started throbbing.

With trembling hands and pounding heart, he did it, his mind racing conjecturing as to what was next.

They both sat opposite corners of the bed.

'So?' the girl asked.

'Umm . . . so?'

'Why did you want me to be here?' she asked and looked at him as if she wanted to see him naked. Tyres, bulges and a sea of fat.

They kicked off their shoes and what I guess, though never told, is that probably they broke the bed. They made out like animals, leaving behind aching love bites and worn out muscles. Saurav had done bloody well for his first time.

He dropped her home that day and the smile never went off his face. The picture he clicked had her kissing him on the cheek while a bed sheet covered their fat naked bodies up to their necks. They kissed and exchanged their byes after which he looked at the picture and cursed himself for clicking just one.

He drove back home speeding all the way through, and shot a mail to his friends with that picture as an attachment. He waited for their replies.

*Bravo! But isn't she a little fat?*

*Cool! Now we are all men in our group.*

*Made for you man! Are you going out with her?*

He smiled and looked at the photograph again. Was he missing her? Already?

The next day, he waited in the car at a distance to catch her before she would enter the gym. He had tasted blood. Quite obviously, he pretty much liked what happened last evening. He put the car in gear as soon as he saw her getting down from the auto and walked towards the gate of the gym.

He screeched the car right in front of her and waved at her.

'What? Are you crazy?'

'Yes, about you,' he shouted. 'Want to go out?'

'Not today,' she said and disappeared inside the gym.

He entered the gym to find her on the same treadmill. She looked at him entering the gym and continued running.

The leg presses felt a little heavy on Saurav legs, as he saw her smiling at the guy running next to her. The wait for the treadmills around her to vacate was getting longer as the conversation between the guy, who was probably the trainer, and Megha was punctuated with laughter and smiles.

Saurav shrugged it off his mind and chose another treadmill and started running as fast he could on. However, the noise and the vibration didn't make her look at him as he had hoped.

After a few bench presses and ball exercises the trainer left her for he had to train a girl who had come in shorts and a bursting sports bra.

'Hi,' Saurav said as he sat down next to Megha.

'Hi.'

'So, what are you doing today?'

'Nothing.'

'So, can we go out and have coffee or something?'

'Or do you want to take me to your place again, huh?'

'Hmmm . . . It is your call. Whatever you want to do.'

'Your place,' she said. Saurav felt something down there. And something up there. He wanted to spell out the word—*Slut*, but he was already panting. They left.

They made out again.

He let his friends know but this time the calls of *slut* and *whore* from his friends hit him. The jibes pinched him.

'Oh . . . You are my man! You have got yourself one horny bitch, man . . . cool! Finally . . . I am so fucking happy for you, man . . . Very nice!'

'At least don't abuse her, man . . .'

'Ooo . . . I am sorry . . . but she *is* one horny girl . . . going to your place two times in two days . . . You are good, man! I am proud of you. Make sure you use a condom dude . . . never know whom she is sleeping with!'

He didn't pursue the conversation any further and decided that that the next day would be a date that doesn't require a place. A bed. Or a pill.

Why? I have never understood Saurav. Make hay while the sun shines. Even when it doesn't. Just go out and make hay. Which perfectly normal guy would prefer a date over a make out session?

The trainer and Megha were laughing their guts out when Saurav reached the gym the next day, slicked hair and in semi-formal clothes. He had dressed up for a date.

The guy left her as his better looking student entered the gym and Saurav made his move.

'What are you doing after this?'

'Nothing? Why? You want me to take me to your place again, you pervert?' she said and giggled.

'No, actually I was thinking maybe we can go out for an early dinner or something?'

'Hmm . . . okay. I will just go and change. But it's on you, right?' she laughed.

She took a shower, changed into her clothes and hugged her trainer before she left the gym with him. Saurav wasn't too happy to see that. It was envy, not love. Saurav was a fat man, the guy was a hunk, probably better in bed. Saurav stood no chance. Flab is never in.

Saurav took her to the most expensive restaurant he had heard of, and I am sure he was thinking of going somewhere which the trainer would not have been able to afford.

It was a nice dimly lit restaurant, probably very classy, and insanely expensive.

'So . . . . What else?' Saurav asked.

'Nothing much.'

'What do you do the whole day?'

'Nothing. I am doing correspondence from Delhi University. So I am at home all the time.' She sipped her lime juice.

'Pretty boring, huh?'

'Yes, but can't help it. That is how I am getting so fat. I just want to get over with my graduation and do an MBA from some place. At least I will get to see a college. It gets so frustrating sitting at home the whole day.'

'Get a boyfriend. That is a nice time pass,' he said that just to check whether she had one and if not, what she thought about having one.

'I already have one,' she looked at him and smiled.

'*You have one?*' Saurav asked, shocked.

'Why do you look so shocked? He is in the US. That is why it is so boring. Had he been here it would not have been that bad.'

He struggled with words as the word *slut* rung in his head. 'What does he do there?'

'Nothing. Doing some course on business or something. He went there to have fun. Nothing else. He is never going to pass it. Whatever.'

'How many years has it been?'

'It will be three next year.'

'So, what are your plans?'

'Nothing. He will come back next year and then within two years we will get married or something. You tell me? Any girl friends? Or is that prohibited in IIT?' she laughed.

'Yes, I have one. She is not in the city . . . Umm . . . she is in Bombay,' he lied.

'So, how much time it has been for you?'

'Just a few months. I don't believe in serious ones.' He didn't know why he said that.

'Me too.'

'Three years and you say you don't believe in serious relationships?'

'I don't. It is just that after a year into any relationship and it is the same. There is a same-ness.'

To this day, Megha remains my best character in the story.

She continued, 'It is just that you fight less in a long term relationship and that is the only parameter of a successful relationship. You get used to that person around you and you don't want to hurt him or her. That is why relationships work. It is like somebody cuts off your cable subscription or internet connections. You throw a fit. But really, after a while everything becomes okay. Yes, when the person you love moves out, there are withdrawal symptoms, but you survive it. Isn't it obvious? You start loving a person more than your best girlfriend in a matter of days and you are ready to leave her for him. It is just that being in love is an idea which is so beautiful. Plus, your girlfriend doesn't have a dick. Your best buddy doesn't have breasts. He won't tell you how good you are. My friend won't tell me how beautiful I look. We need someone from the opposite sex to do it, to satisfy our ego, our needs. That is what love is: a desperate need to feel good. Love is an illusion, nothing more, nothing less.'

Ever since I have heard this from Saurav, I have used this speech more than a few times on broken hearted girlfriends and distraught boyfriends. The guys start looking for someone better. The girls don't understand.

'So you don't love him?'

'I don't know. It just feels nice sometimes that he is there. Plus, instead of marrying someone you don't know, I would rather marry him. He is an okay person, doesn't drink or smoke. He will join his father's business and has a secured future. He loves me too, I guess. So, I don't think it is too bad a deal.'

'*Deal?*'

'Yes, why not? Arranged marriages are deals, aren't they? You choose the best possible match. A compromise between looks, family background and economic strength is struck and then you marry him or her. This isn't any different. He is the best I could have got with all the flab hanging around. I am set for life.'

Saurav had nothing to say. I had nothing to say when Saurav narrated this to me. Had he described her to me as someone even remotely sexy, I would have fallen in love.

'Okay.'

'I am sorry for that. I just said what I wanted to say.'

'I think you made sense,' he said. Saurav, at this point, had started comparing himself to her guy.

'Shall we leave? Mom would be expecting me.'

'Sure.'

Saurav dropped her home and told her that he had a good time. She repeated the same.

He went home that day and deleted the picture from his cell phone and computer. He didn't have the heart to delete it from there.

Calling her a slut a million times in his head didn't count as he thought he was falling harder for her with every passing second. He was damn lucky he came across her or he would have still been a virgin.

Saurav missed the gym next day as his internship had started.

He called her from his office but she did not pick. The gym trainer's image kept cropping in his head while he sleepwalked through all the sessions organized for him that day. He kept calling and messaging her throughout the day and she did not revert even once.

The next day, he missed office and went to see her at the gym. She seemed to be having a good time with the trainer, laughing and blabbing with him. Saurav's temper rose, but he still walked up casually to the closest couch and sat down there.

After the trainer got up and attended the thinner sexier girls, Saurav came up to her.

'Hi'

'Hi,' she said as she grabbed her things and walked past him.

'You have not been picking up my calls.'

'I know,' she said as they walked out of the gym.

'Why not? Did I offend you anyway?'

'I was busy,' she said casually not looking at him.

'You could have sent one message.'

'I didn't get time,' she said coldly.

'For *one* message?'

'No, I mean I was really busy. Don't irritate me.'

'Where were you busy?' he asked as they both paced towards an auto.

'My boyfriend was in town, I had a late night the day before and was very tired the next day.'

'And yesterday? You were tired the whole day?'

'I went out with Amit,' she said as she haggled with the auto driver.

'Amit?'

'The trainer.'

'You went out with him? Why? *Why?* I mean, you see how he flirts with all the girls in the gym. He is not a nice person. How can you even talk to him? '

'Look, Saurav. Don't tell me what to do.' She got inside the auto. 'And let me decide who is nice and who is not. I am doing whatever I want to. I am not answerable to you.'

'You just slept with me. Yes, you are. I love you.'

'No you don't.'

'Yes, I do,' he said frantically.

'Buzz off.'

'You want a deal, right? I am richer than your guy. I am an IITian for heaven's sake. I will be with you.'

'Are you drunk?'

'No, I love you.'

'No, you don't. You think you do because we made out. But you don't.'

The auto had left him leaving behind a cloud of dust and haze. Saurav told me he felt really stupid after that.

He stopped going to the gym. Deleted her number. Deleted her picture. He had no choice after she had stopped picking his calls and changed her gym timings and the gym people would not let him know when she came.

Time flew by and he forgot about her.

The twist came after two months when she called Saurav and told him that she had broken up. She asked if they could meet up and Saurav turned it down, though the prospect of making out again was almost too tempting.

Maybe Saurav was the second most lucrative deal in town as it was certain she would not go after the trainer with a Hero Honda bike. Anyway, it did not work out in her favour.

Whatever happened, it did good to Saurav, though. He had done it before twenty four. Hail Freud!

He got close to getting into a relationship a couple of times after that. He almost kissed one. The first girlfriend, the first love, the first boyfriend, and the first fling. Take these seriously. Good learning ground, I always say. I learnt how not to get dumped. It is amazing how many different ways you can get dumped. I know six from experience.

Anyway, Saurav at least learnt something. *Don't* go out on dates when you can have it three times on three days. You never know when times change.

However, he still thought about her but that was only when he had to fantasize.

# Garima—Beautiful, Rich, Foolish

Garima was sitting in her room when the results were announced. She looked out of the window.

Hyderabad.

She went back to scratching her chipped black nail paint off her fingers. It had been three years her nails had seen any other colour. No, she wasn't a heavy metal fan. She wasn't a punk either, though her sheer disdain towards dressing up and an affinity towards the colour black suggested otherwise. She used to wear unflattering loose T-shirts with dirty jeans and *chappals* to go with. Her frizzy brown hair was always left open and her eyes always had kohl smeared carelessly by her roommate Aditi. The same girl who used to do all Garima's shopping, overloading her wardrobe with all the girly stuff that she never wore, getting her accessories that she never put on. But Garima never stopped her from doing so. If not she, at least Aditi felt good about it. Aditi had tried more than a million times to draw her out of her quietness, but in the last three years, nothing yielded. Yes, Garima was the life of many parties, getting drunk and dancing the night out, but that was the only socializing she ever did. *Getting drunk.*

She never made any friends. She never wanted to. She was

fine with the emptiness around her, no matter how many people wanted to get close to her. She was a nice person otherwise, helping anyone who needed to be helped. But that didn't mean she would be friends with them.

There were a lot of things to like her for, in her: her smile, which she flashed only if someone did anything stupid, her face, beyond the *kohl*, fair as the moon and glowing, her dark brown hair that she never thought about cutting. Guys often fell for her, but the thought that she was going to abuse them soon used to break their hearts into a million pieces.

She wasn't like this from always. She used to be a girl. A normal one.

Everybody has breakups. So what if she had one?

That is what everyone said. Garima, about three years ago and days after her board results came out, had caught Karan kissing some other girl, right in front of her eyes.

She could have got into any college in Delhi. She chose Chennai. Away from her home, friends, the few she had, her family and Karan.

Her family resisted, but they couldn't stop her from going. She was never refused anything by her family. She was born after her mother's earlier pregnancy ended in a stillborn twin brother and sister. When she came into the family, their business saw money like it had never seen before and she was always thought the reason behind it. She was loved beyond measure by everyone in her family and her word was the first priority. Despite all this, she was hardly spoilt, her demands rarely extravagant.

In fact, she rarely asked for anything and took the bus to school like everyone else, while her Honda CRV and her driver rotted in the garage. Karan took the same bus every day and they sat together. Till the time Karan thought it would be better if they went to school in her car. It would give them more time together, he said.

Whatever happened between Karan and Garima was never privy to them, as no matter what it was, Garima never hid things from her mother. Right from the day when Karan asked her out on Valentine's Day to the day he had first held her hand, everything was known to her. The subsequent things were quite obviously never discussed, though her mother politely asked her to be careful.

Her mother never liked Karan, but she never had the heart to tell Garima so. She was the happiest when Karan proposed to her and her mother was happy to see her daughter smiling and hopping about. The next day, Garima gifted Karan a gleaming new cell phone. Her mother said nothing.

They were so much in love. Or maybe only she was. Karan never reciprocated as much as Garima did, but then he couldn't possibly match up, Garima thought, as she loved him so much. Karan came from an upper middle class family while she was filthy rich. Garima had her own credit card before she was fifteen.

Everybody knew about the two of them. An ideal couple. Garima was tall, fair and had fuzzy long hair which reached a few inches below her neck. She stood tall. She had inherited it from her mother and the hours spent at the basketball court had toned her body to a bikini perfect state. Awesomely toned legs, a perfect bosom, dark brown almond eyes and a flawless complexion, completed the picture. She was one of the fuller girls. Just the right weight. A girl you would like to hug. And do some dirty things with. Pictures of her in a basketball jersey and shorts made you want to indulge in some tiring activities. Not all of them being basketball.

And by what I know about Karan, he was pretty good looking too. But whatever.

They were envied, praised and loved.

They were both extremely brainy and often fought for the top position in class. The time that Karan spent at her home often rivalled the time he spent in his own. Her parents were slightly miffed at her, when Karan and she spent hours sitting in her room with a shut door and were supposedly studying but they said nothing because they had nothing against Karan. Nobody had anything against Karan. He was feet-touching, high scoring good looking kid whom everybody loved, from teachers, to friends' parents to grandparents.

Though he never did anything out of the ordinary, he never pulled back his words on how much he loved her, and how much he wanted to be with her. He was very smart in these matters.

Anyway, no matter what everyone thought, Garima did every ridiculous thing in the book to keep him happy. One casual mention about the PlayStation his friend Ketan had got himself and the next month anniversary, he got that in his hands. No matter how fervently he tried to keep her from giving him these gifts, Garima relentlessly made sure he kept them.

As months passed, Garima's life started revolving around Karan. She, who once, had friends all over her place, all the time, had just one name governing everything in her life. The friends were slowly left behind, the groups she was in, continued without her and she didn't have any problem with it. She spent her days sitting at home and thinking about him. Garima stopped seeing any point in going out with her friends who didn't interest her anymore. All she thought about was him. She woke up with his name on her lips and slept with his name in her heart. Her heart still skipped a beat when she used to see his name on the phone. Garima slept every night clutching the cell phone in her hand, just in case he called.

Her pulse peaked whenever he said he loved her. The world seemed a much nicer place when he was around.

She never wanted anything from him. She was just glad the Karan was around to take care of her. Karan worked on extremes. He ignored her right to the point where she would be moments away from tears. And when that happened, he used to come up with great lines and some flowers to make her fall in love with him harder.

It works wonders. It gets most dividends. Get your girls used to loads of attention all the time and they will not value it. Make them get used to the uncaring you, so that when you do show them love, it would pay. In gifts. Kisses. Hugs. More.

Prerna, her best friend once, now only friend, often warned her against her obsession with Karan, though it hardly mattered. Best girl friends have always been the biggest enemies of dirty boyfriends.

'Garima, I think you are going too far,' she said on her now very infrequent visits to her place. Garima had stopped going out unless it was with Karan. Though, he preferred staying at home . . . for obvious reasons.

'Why, Prerna?' Girls often lose all senses of reason in love.

'*Why?* Which girlfriend gives her boyfriend such an expensive watch? It is ridiculous.'

'But he wanted it, Prerna. He wanted it so much.'

'Guys want everything. You can't go on giving him anything. Tomorrow he will drool after a BMW and are you will buy him that too?'

'I will buy him whatever I want to. And yes, if I have that kind of money, I will buy him everything that he wants. It is my money, why do you care?'

'You are so rude,' Prerna said, as she gathered her books to leave.

'So are you.'

'See, Garima, I have nothing against you. All I want to tell you is to be careful with Karan. He has been showing things off that you bought him, as his own. And this I know for sure. That iPod you gave him, he denied that you had given him. Mom swear. But you do whatever you feel like. Just that, he was also spotted with Ritika, the one from the science section a couple of times. Just open your eyes.'

'Whatever,' Garima said and stared at her book, her eyes already turning away from even the thought of it.

'Whatever.'

Prerna left.

Garima had started crying. She was unimaginably angry at whatever Prerna had just said. She was already imagining him with her.

I don't know Karan, but why would anyone, I mean *anyone*, leave a hot, rich, girlfriend who lets you in to her bedroom, to go out with some average looking girl? We are a strange species. Us, men.

Going back to that day, Garima sat there crying, weighing whether she should ask him about Ritika. After an hour of deliberation, she called up Karan, who kept rejecting her calls as he said he would. It was Garima's birthday and the board result celebration on the next day and he had said he would be busy preparing for it.

She called up his friends and the third one gave the venue of the surprise party away. The place was a five minute drive away and Garima drove to that place in her night suit only to regret doing so.

She caught Karan in the parking lot with Ritika.

Kissing.

No matter what Karan did afterwards it made no difference to her. She was leaving for Chennai. Three years away from her home, that house, that city, that bedroom, that car, in fact the world she lived in.

Away from everything.

It was only after the break up, that she realized she loved him more than she had ever imagined. She cried for days, stopped eating and harboured suicidal tendencies. She felt used. Cheated, she was.

Her world had crashed right in front of her eyes.

She thought it would take a lifetime to build it again. She was wrong.

Love is not what you live for. Love is what makes it a little easier.

# Silverman Financial: The First Day

Monday, 4th August.

8: 00 am

*I will not bathe.*

Snooze.

8:10 am

*I will not shave.*

Snooze.

8: 20 am

*I will take a cab.*

Snooze.

8: 30 am

*What the fuck?*

Turns off alarm.

9: 30am.

*'Great. Up before the alarm. Not bad for the first day.'*

Saurav told himself and reached out for his cell phone. A swanky new N96, a phone he had seen the Roadies, the bickering contestants of a popular reality television show, carry. He wondered why his phone said six miss calls. Then he saw, the small clock on the top of the screen.

**9:40.**

*9:40?*

*What the fuck?*

*How is this possible?*

The alarm didn't ring; he was sure.

He got up in a flash, cursing the phone for its meek, powerless bullshit speakers.

'Does it have FM and alarm?' That's what his mom asked him when he had bought this brick sized phone and told her about the GPS navigation system. If only he had taken her seriously.

He shaved. He took a bath. He couldn't afford to look bad; he wanted all the attention he could get from the girls on him. He had seen awesomely sexy banker girls in the movies. He couldn't possibly miss out on them!

He put on his new white and blue striped Zodiac shirt. He slipped into his pin striped Blackberry trousers. A blue Bentley tie.

Saurav had lost a lot of weight since the days of Megha, but you still wouldn't call him thin, fit or anywhere near that.

He patted his paunch and cursed IIT for it had made him fat, which it had, checked his tie for the last time, and ordered a cab. He kept his hands away from the sandwich which was left over from yesterday. Today was the millionth time he thought he would start dieting from.

He was ready for his first day at office.

And was late by 45minutes. Already.

10: 15 am.

The cab would still take fifteen minutes.

Last week had been a wild goose chase across the length and breadth of the city to find a suitable house. So much so, that it almost spoilt the whole fun of staying at Taj Banjara, the last word in luxury hotels. Paid in full by Silverman.

Three gyms, two pools, breakfast buffets, super-hot Hotel Management grads, et all! He had asked a few of the house keeping staff for their number, but it didn't happen.

Even saying that he was an IIT graduate didn't help. *Sluts*, he told himself.

To get back at them he stuffed all the shampoos, soaps and combs into his bag before he left the hotel.

Anyway, he had managed a flat, at walking distance from that hotel, quite ironically.

Saurav had already started missing Delhi and the beautiful Delhi girls. They were more receptive to *I-am-from-IIT-Delhi*.

*'Naye ho, sahab?'*

*'Haan.'*

'Twenty minutes to reach there,' he said with a typical Hyderabadi accent.

'Just be a little quick,' he said as he opened the newspaper. It was a great feeling. Only if the car would have been a Lexus and his own. He had refused the car his dad offered to take to Hyderabad saying that he was good enough to buy one of his own!

He put the newspaper aside and started fiddling with his phone. A good thirty minutes later they reached a maze of huge buildings and wide roads.

If Delhi traffic was bad, this was worse. Nobody shouted or charged at each other with iron rods but they were pretty much banging into each other all the time!

10:45 am.

He was an hour and a half late. It was 11 a.m. when he saw the building from a distance.

The building was as humungous as it was beautiful. Steel and curved glass formed an imposing structure. Its monstrosity made him feel so terribly insignificant. I remember going through the same emotion. A big building. A taller woman. They all do that to you, the intimidate you.

As they approached the entrance, the top of the building was no longer visible.

A few honks from cars nearby and a smug faced guard appeared and said something foul in a south Indian language. Saurav too abused, just to retort.

'*Sahab*, you have to get down outside only. Only personal cars allowed,' the cabby said.

Saurav got down and he drove the car away.

Seven hundred and fifty bucks for a cab ride and he would still be seen walking to the office.

He still wasn't out of the awe of the building when he saw something else which left a lasting impression on his mind.

*The Driveway.*

The car right behind him was an Audi.

The car right behind the Audi was a BMW 7 series.

The car next to it was a Mercedes C class.

And the car which almost banged into it, Honda CRV.

He would buy the Audi, he made up his mind. He was not a big fan of European cars.

An hour earlier, Abhi was standing where Saurav did now.

Abhi had stood outside the door for a few seconds, taken a deep breath and let it out. It was a new *him* entering through those doors, those doors that led him to a new life, which had fame, success and money at every step.

Saurav swung open the revolving door and strode in with a big smile, looked at everybody who walked past and smiled at them. I remember *seeing* him then. He looked funny. And fat.

After a few seconds of awkwardly looking at the huge empty space in front of him, with his mouth half open, he started looking for the reception. The ceiling of Silverman Finance is about twenty feet high and the place is brightly lit in a brownish yellowish glow accentuated by the same coloured marble below. It is an insanely huge hall.

One walk around the Silverman office and you start feeling small. There is a whole city inside it.

He walked up to the far corner of the huge hall, where the reception was.

Saurav peered across the huge wooden desk, shining as if polished just a moment ago, behind which, were seven people manning it, headsets on their ears and a big smile over their faces. All of them beautiful, their lips shone with gloss.

A big sign hung overhead, with bright yellow lights shining behind it.

**SILVERMAN FINANCIAL**

'Excuse me. I am Saurav and . . .'

'Good morning Saurav. Here is your access card. Go straight take and a left. Swipe your card, this way up, there. Take the lift to the second floor. Go straight and take the third right. You will reach the training room.'

He thought of asking for her number but she had gone back staring at her computer screen.

He crossed the waiting area which was more like a movie

theatre, only that the seats were much better and the LCD screens were a shade smaller. He stood there, eyes fixed on the screen watching CNBC, just because the ambience was so riveting. He craved for popcorn.

Just as he was about to lose all sense of time, he was knocked right in by the hurried *clicking clocking* of high heeled women and Cuban-heeled men all around him. It was a sea of expensive fabric, banned leather and exotic perfumes. People glided across the floor in Hugo Boss*es*, Armani*s* and Versace*s* with Louis Vuitton either hanging from their shoulders or making their feet look beautiful.

Of whatever Saurav knew about brands, he picked up the most expensive of clothes that Connaught Place had to offer, but they were made to look like tatters. Everyone was tall, insanely well built, immaculately dressed and most of them looked American or European with a tan gone wrong.

Women had their hair tied tightly behind their heads, making their skin seem like a taut membrane stretched over their cheek bones. This smoothed out their wrinkles. As for the men, their suits shone, their shoes glistened and their watches glimmered. Their heads shone. Some of them were half bald. Rest had theirs slicked with gel in a great hairstyle. They had sacks full of money to spare and they spent it well.

He cursed the men, and wished the women were naked. He smiled at them and they looked at him with disgusted looks on their faces.

He swiped his card, rotated the stiles and entered the lift lobby.

Twelve lifts, six on each side, a few of them opened, a few closed. The whole floor was sparkling clean. Brown marble, golden plated lifts glistened in the neon lighting. Huge mirrors covered the walls.

He chose the lift with the fewest people in. The lift was a

room in itself. There a two-seater sofa right there. *For making out?*

While he waited restlessly for the lift to reach the third floor, people around him were busy digging into their BlackBerries and PDAs.

The lift reached the third floor and he breathed easy.

He left the lift lobby and saw the figures he had seen at the ground floor. They were sitting amongst a sea of the same kind of people, with their eyes glued on to their computer screens. Nothing moved, no one talked. Yoga sessions are louder.

Saurav remembered the instructions. He walked straight towards the training room. No longer what he was wearing on his wrist or on himself was exclusive or above par. Everything was pedestrian, his phone was an embarrassment now. His shoes, a joke. His slight paunch, a calamity.

He rushed across the floor, taking small but fast strides eyes on his feet, trying to avoid attracting attention. A penguin among humans.

He felt more eyes turning on to him, sighing and turning away.

Saurav finally felt relieved when he saw in bold letters.

***Training Room***

# The Second Day At Training: Sumita Kicks Some Serious Ass

The second day of training had started on a very peaceful note, unlike the first, when a stern looking female who stood three inches taller than Saurav, asked him to go back home as being late was something which was not tolerated. He had to leave the room and the office building. Not quite the start he was looking for.

That day, he was the only person sitting in the room, fifteen minutes early.

A few minutes later, a few badly dressed men and women—boys and girls, more precisely—walked in, fidgeting with their hair and watches.

Within the next fifteen minutes, the room was filled with twenty people selected from twenty elite colleges. All of them were over-achievers.

The conversation between them shifted swiftly from how much they had scored in their graduation to the bigger things they had achieved in their lives. The Stephen's College girl had forgone masters at LSE to join Silverman Finance. The IIT Mumbai graduate was an IIM (A) dropout.

One IITian had a patent to his name; something called a brain oximeter and wanted to look for investors in the company.

The girl from Delhi College of Engineering was a national badminton champion, apart from being a gold medallist in various Olympiads, both national and international.

The girl from Presidency was super cute.

An easy silence hung in the room. Everybody was trying to keep conversation to the minimum. I wouldn't be telling you this story had Abhi not picked the seat next to Saurav.

The whispers died down and everybody sat up in their chairs as a clicking-clocking sound approached the door. Saurav wanted to ask Abhi if the same female who had come the previous day would come that today too, but pulled back seeing him freeze.

She walked in.

Sumita Bhasin. Chief HR. Silverman Finance.

Her perfume invaded their nostrils and violated their sense of smell. What Saurav hadn't seen the day before, he could see then. Sumita was colossal, almost twice in every dimension of an average Indian woman. Or man. She leaned over the table they were sitting on and ran her eyes through the room.

'Seems like everybody is present today,' she said, smiled and showed her big teeth jutting out from blackened gums.

Saurav momentarily made eye contact with her. He wanted to fart on her face.

Sumita was approaching fifty and was fighting hard to keep it away. She had the familiar hairstyle that let her hide her wrinkles. Her wrinkles were not done in by the monthly Botox shots she took, which bloated her foot long face and made it look even more sinister. She hardly smiled; the last plastic surgery which stretched her skin from nose downwards had left little scope to do that. She stood taller and was wider than most men around her, especially with a four inch pencil heels, which over the years had made her veins, jut out from her feet.

Sumita had been working in the firm since its inception and swore by the company rules. Very tight ass. She tolerated no slip ups and made life hell for whoever did so. She wielded almost absolute power and had to just go one level up to get anybody she wanted out of the company. Her voice was raspy, her words, harsh. There was not one girl who hadn't been reduced to tears by her cutting words. The men had it no better.

She called for an office boy who got twenty hundred-paged manuals for them.

**Campus to Corporate**, it said in bold letters.

'I want you to go through it before we proceed,' she said, her voice seemed like a man's baritone, grated over a cheese grater, it sounded like she had a perennial cold. But that took nothing away from it, in terms of volume. When she whispered, the whole office could hear what she had to say.

They started flipping through the pages. Most of them started underlining what they thought was important. Geeks!

But no one dared to smile.

It was a detailed account of how they were expected to behave at SF, how they were expected to dress up, how they were to address people and the like. It even had addresses of places they could buy their clothes from. Silverman had a design consultant for clothes right in their office.

Saurav started nudging Abhi to show him something he found amusing and Abhi asked him to shut up a little more loudly than he would have liked to.

'You think it is funny?' Bhasin asked scornfully, pointing at them.

'Who? Me?' Abhi said, already sweating all over.

'Yes,' she said, hands on her waist, head leaned forward, her eyebrows making a hill on her forehead and anger writ large on her face.

'I was reading it, ma'am.'

'First lesson you learn at Silverman Finance,' she leaned back and looked at all of us. 'We are smarter than you. And every joke played here is on you. Not us.' She reverted her stare back to Abhi and asked, 'What did you find funny, Mr Abhi Gupta?'

'Nothing, ma'am.'

'What did you find difficult enough not to be understood on your own?' she asked, and her voice rose with every sentence.

'Nothing, ma'am.'

'Out of the room.'

'Ma'am?'

'Did you not hear me, Mr Gupta? You think we are all fools here to have made this manual. Look at yourself. Does anybody here think he looks like the people working outside? They are all professionals there. You have to be like them. And it is my job to get you there. There or out of here. ' She banged the manual on the table.

'But . . . '

'It was me, I was asking—' Saurav butted in.

'OUT!' She pointed towards the door. 'Leave the building. Right now. And that is for both of you.'

'Okay,' Saurav said and promptly collected his stuff to leave. Abhi had no choice but to follow him out of the room.

'If you still behave like college kids, this is how we are going to treat you. The only difference is you lose a job here and not some grades. It's up to you.' She stared at them, waiting for the fear to register.

'To start with, let me tell you very honestly,' she said and got up from her chair. 'Each one of you today, here, is a disgrace to our company.' She smiled to show all of her upper jaw, and rubbed her hands together. Her long red painted nails shone.

'Every one of you may have topped your college, but that accounts for nothing. We are all toppers. And that's our minimum criteria. *You* would not be here if you were not. Anyway, now that you are here, there are just a few simple rules that you need to follow. They are given in this manual.'

'I assume that  nobody gets these things now,' she said and continued, 'However there is one advice that you could make good use of. Every slip costs us. We don't tolerate that. We are giving you money that nobody else does. We expect that back. And more. That is business. The day you slip, it would be good for you to update your CVs and look for new jobs. We do not tolerate incompetence. Only the best stay. The best are very few. Thank you and have a great day ahead. And if Mr Abhi or Mr Saurav talks to anyone of you, tell them they have already taken a step in the wrong direction. Out of this place.'

She picked up her handbag and left. They stared at each other, red faced as they thought about what she had just said.

The training lectures started.

It was 10 a.m. then. They sat in the same damned position for the next sixteen hours, except for an hour each for lunch and dinner. It was getting tough even for people who were used to studying sixteen hours a day. These were the people who were academically the most brilliant in the country. These were the most tireless and intelligent brains of the country and they were tired out by Silverman in a single day.

By the time that day got over, it was 2 a.m. Their asses were stiff and most of them wished that day was an exception, not the norm. They had heard about demanding schedules of Investment Banks, but they had no idea the rigor would start so soon.

Silverman wasn't going to pay them for doing a nine to five, cushy job. They wanted the last cell of their bodies to work for them till it died and decayed.

The only good thing left about the job was the paycheque, now that they knew they would be working their asses off for it.

Apparently not.

After they were thrown out, while Abhi was embarrassed and felt like sitting and brooding over it, Saurav was already in the lift lobby. He waved at Abhi like a madman.

Abhi walked up to him, head bowed as he thought about what had just happened. It wouldn't do much good to his days there, he thought.

'I am really sorry for that. That bitch . . .' Saurav said as they both entered the lift.

'It's fine. Not entirely your fault.'

'Saurav.' He put his hand out.

'Abhi.' They shook hands.

'Where do you live?'

'Madapur.'

'Okay.' A few more minutes of silence passed between them. 'Is there a problem?' Saurav asked him.

'No,' Abhi said, still not looking.

'I am sorry for what happened in there.'

'So am I.'

'I tried to take you out. It didn't work out.'

'I know.'

'Why are you so pissed off then?'

'Am I?'

'Yes, you are. Totally.'

'So what do you want?'

'Nothing.' Saurav was a little taken back at the rudeness of the whole conversation.

'Great.'

'Do you drink?' he asked, almost mocking.

'Occasionally,' Abhi said, looking up for the first time in the whole conversation.

'Let's go.'

'On you,' Abhi said.

Saurav invited him to his place and Abhi spent five minutes gawking at the huge flat.

Abhi's place opened with a washroom on the left and a kitchen on the right. And had two tiny rooms and three people shared it.

Saurav had an ice box with two crates of beer in it, with every single beer in place. He was adhering to his crash diet.

They clinked their bottles and after the first bottle, they were a little tipsy, both of them being non-drinkers. 'Do you drink often? This crate . . .?' Abhi asked, with bloodshot eyes.

'Looks good to have an ice box and everything. Very occasional. So you tell me, why did you get so worked up today?'

'Nothing. It was just . . .'

'Yes?'

'It is just that, I really want to make it big here. This is my chance. Get rich. Have a house like this, you know. This job means everything to me,' Abhi said with exaggerated hand movements.

'C'mon Abhi, if not this then something else. There are a million jobs out there, man.' Saurav took another swig at the bottle.

'I am not an IITian like you. Nobody is dying to take us in. Jobs come far and few. And ones like these? Once in a lifetime. I lose this, twenty years of slogging goes down the drain. I will be just like any other graduate.'

Saurav smiled inside on hearing the IIT part and said, 'What crap? You are good, you are intelligent. You would get through a good one . . . .'

'My dad, college topper. What does he do? Works for the government. Earns peanuts. Why? He didn't take chances. Or lost them. I am not going to do that. I will make this work come what may. I will have three cars in my driveway before thirty, have rings on all my fingers and have three servants serving me while my wife blows all my money in a beauty parlour. When people look at me, I want them to crave for a life like mine. I want them to wish they were as rich as me.'

'Hmmm . . . here for the money?'

'Yes. Loads of it.'

'People would call you greedy.'

'People who already have three cars.'

'I have three cars.'

'You do?'

'Four actually.'

'Really?'

'Yes.'

'So you think I am greedy?'

'I don't know.'

'No, say it.'

'I don't know.'

Saurav got up and made him sit down as Abhi was finding it hard to stand without holding on to something.

'Thanks Saurav. But remember, someday I too will have

four in my drive way.'

'I am sure you will,' Saurav said and made him lie down on the couch.

'And have three girlfriends.'

'You can have them now.'

'No. You need money for that.'

'No, you don't,' Saurav said.

'You do. They all love that. Money. I too . . . want a rich girlfriend . . . with loads of money.'

He flopped on the bed and fell fast asleep.

The next day was a holiday. It was *Guru Purnima.*

*Report to office today.*
*Extra lecture sessions.*
*Thank you.*
*—Sumita Bhasin.*

They missed the message in their beer-induced sleep.

They had expected it but somehow they still wished it wouldn't happen. They were called up by Sumita in her cubicle and given an earful for missing office the day before, without informing anyone. Apparently, the cab waited fifteen minutes for them. They were called irresponsible, unprofessional and everything that could be said in the limits of office decency and were reminded that their days might just be limited in Silverman.

The training classes only got more exhausting after the first day. Going to office became a drag and they lived their lives from one Sunday to another. Their life was reduced to an unchanging back-breaking schedule. Get up at seven, reach office by eight, attend lectures till two in the night, come back home and sleep. They had absolutely no time left for anything else. The two weekends that went past were consumed by sleep. Their frustrations crept up by each passing second. But they had no choice; this was the life they had chosen for themselves. It was two weeks to their first salary and that was the only thing they looked forward to. At least they were being paid amply for all that they were going through. It would all be worth it after they got the pay cheque, they'd thought.

Two and half lakhs. Both of them had plans. Saurav had eyes on a Tissot watch. Abhi wanted to gift his parents a foreign holiday. Still, they would have enough to last six months.

Life was about to get better.

Or maybe not.

# All That Glitters Is Not Silver

It was the last day of their second week in Silverman. Just as they got up to leave, a sweet looking man from the HR department came and addressed everybody in a very sweet tone, rubbing his hands together and smiling ear to ear.

'Good evening, everybody. I am Tarun, from the HR department. I hope you have had a good time up till now. And that we have come up to your expectations.'

Nobody answered.

'Seems like all of you are very tired, so I will come straight to what I need to tell you. As you know, Silverman has very high standards and strict quality guidelines, and it is expected that you reach that level. Since you are all fresh out of college, you have a lot to learn and imbibe in terms of knowledge as well as how the corporate environment works, it is decided by the management, purely because all of you are very raw and inexperienced, and not because you are not worthy enough, to put you all in an advanced internship programme.'

Everybody woke up and listened.

'It is nothing to worry about. It's just a standard procedure. The internship programme is nothing but an evaluation of where you stand and how have you worked in the last six months.' People started looking at each other and tried to find someone who was not surprised and knew what this was all about. Everybody sat up, all eyes set on him, hearts in their mouths.

He continued, 'After six months, every one of you will be evaluated and only then will you be a permanent employee in this firm. Few of you will have to bid your byes to the firm . . . that is only if you don't perform.'

Their pulses took a shot upwards. They were being pitted against each other. Their hearts sank and they started to sweat. They were being evaluated.

*'Bullshit,'* Saurav said out loud.

'Quiet class. If you have any questions, Ms Sumita Bhasin will clear them out. But first somebody will come and give you the letter that stipulates all the conditions of the internship. Go through it. And yes, till the time you don't clear the programme, the remuneration given to you will be just your basic salary. That's since you would be under the training module and not essentially adding anything to the company. Thank you for your time. Everything is in that letter. Do go through it.' He left and closed the door behind him. It was followed with a pin drop silence in the class.

The circular was distributed.

The revised salary was seven lakhs. Their basic salary, down from the thirty they had been offered. No watches. No holidays.

Everybody sat with head hung low, as they thought about what lay in front. Seven lakhs, of the thirty promised.

It wasn't worth it anymore. Twenty odd years of hard work had withered these people away. Each one of them had spent days brooding behind closed doors whenever they came in second. Cursing themselves for every mistake they made. Every exam they didn't top. Every medal they missed.

All they had accumulated all these years were some papers with numbers on it, a few medals, a few certificates. This was the time all that hard work would have meant something. They felt robbed.

They deserved what they had been promised.

They were crushed. The last six months they day-dreamed about this day, when the last many years' hard work would pay off and it will be all even . . . They missed movies, they missed friendships, the missed relationships, they missed parties, and they deprived themselves of all the fun for this one day. The day they would race ahead of the lot. The day it would all be even. However, it did not happen. Their dreams were shattered, their hopes crushed. They had not just taken their promised salary away, but also twenty years of their lives away.

Shoulders drooped. The girls were close to tears. Some cried while the others started crying in a bid to console them. Some leaned back into their chairs, slouched and ran over the last the six months in which they did nothing but think about this day.

Abhi sat there open mouthed. He felt cheated. Humiliated. Saurav kept swearing.

Abhi didn't even have the heart to tell his mom about this.

The only consolation was that a month later a few of them were to be taken to Singapore for a training schedule. That gladdened them, but the words *few* reminded them of the choppy waters that lay ahead. The person next to them could cost them their job.

Before people could start knowing each other, a big wall was drawn up between them. Everyone was competition now. The field was set.

'Wonder how much I would be earning had I not been greedy,' Abhi looked at the ceiling and sighed.

The second guy in his old class would be earning more than him.

'Hmm . . .' Saurav said as he looked around to see faces hung in disappointment.

Everyone wanted the money. That is what jobs are for. Money.

Of all the new joinees, it was Shruti who went through the letter most frantically. Time and time again.

'Unfair,' Garima said and rocked in her chair.

'Huh?' Shruti said, her mind still blank.

'It is very unfair.'

'Yes,' she said, her eyes wet.

'We could have done better. A lot better.'

The class started leaving. Garima waited for Shruti to say something, but Shruti just stared at the letter as her eyes got wetter. She didn't even blink.

'Are you okay?'

The whole class had left but Shruti kept sitting there. Like a corpse. 'Yes,' she said.

'You want to me to bring you something. Water?' Garima handed over a bottle to her. Shruti broke down, dug her head inside her palms and started to weep bitterly.

Garima put her hand on her head and tapped it soothingly. Half an hour passed by the time she stopped crying.

'Thank you,' Shruti said.

'For?'

'I don't know.' Shruti walked, still dazed. She stumbled over chairs.

'Are you sure you are okay? You don't look fine to me.'

'Huh?'

'You want to sit in the cafeteria?'

'I don't want to stay here.'

'Come to my place,' Garima said.

'My parents won't allow that.'

'They don't have to know.'

Both of them headed to her place and Garima gave her pyjamas to wear. Garima asked her to choose a top for herself from the wardrobe.

Shruti peeked in the wardrobe and for the first time that evening, her expression changed. It got a twinkle to her eye.

She stood there, rummaging through the tonnes of fabric Garima had stashed in her cupboard.

'Like something?' Garima asked apologetically.

'I like *everything*. I have never worn anything so . . . nice . . . and expensive . . . You really have a nice taste.'

'My friend does. She bought it for me. Never wore much of it.'

Garima noticed that everything Shruti wore was stitched. No labels. But she still managed to look smashing. The pyjama she gave Shruti seemed like it was made for her. Not that Garima was fat, she was miles away from it, but she lacked the tone Shruti's body had. And she lacked the brown chocolate fantasy complexion. Smoking had grown Garima thin. The household chores had got Shruti thin.

'You can have anything you want.' Garima said. She felt a sudden surge of liking towards Shruti. She spent the next hour dressing Shruti up in the finest of her tops and dresses and felt good about it. Shruti obviously had no qualms about getting into clothes she had never dreamt of.

Two girls who can share clothes and be happy about it, is the best example of selfless friendship you can ever get.

Beyond everything, the only thing I thought about when they narrated me this incident was whether Shruti changed in front of Garima or not.

Tired, both of them lay down on the bed.

'You can keep anything you want to.'

'I can't just take it like that. They are yours,' Shruti said even though she wanted to say yes.

'You can. I don't wear them anyway,' she said as she lit up a cigarette.

'Why do you smoke?'

'I like to.'

'Why?'

'That way, you don't have to talk to people around.'

'I should stop talking then,' Shruti said.

'Hmm . . .' She stubbed the cigarette. 'So, talk.'

'Conversation is a two way street. You have to talk too, just in case . . .'

'Start.'

Shruti spent the night telling her about everything she had gone through. Garima cried more than once as she told Shruti about Karan and told her how she always thought life was unfair to her.

Garima told her not to worry about anything and that things would be alright. Garima woke up the next day to a hot cup of coffee, French toast and freshly cut fruits. For Shruti, it was a way of life. They went out shopping that day, Shruti wanted to dust Garima's place but Garima insisted they go out.

'That is looking great . . . that blue really suits you.'

'It does?'

'Really nice. Girls wear that sort of stuff these days.'

'You are a girl.'

'Nice girls.'

'You are a nice girl.'

'I mean . . . girly girls . . . I don't like dressing up.'

'Why not? You would look much better than you look in those loose jeans and the dull oversized T-shirt.'

'There is no one to dress up for. Try this . . .' She handed her something yellow.

'Find someone . . .' Shruti shouted over the dressing room and laughed. 'How is this?'

'Great. We will take both,' Garima said.

'What? I can't buy this.'

'I am getting you this.'

'Garima . . . I don't want you to pay . . .'

'Zip it. Just this time . . . Get a guy the next time.'

'Yes . . . right,' Shruti said sarcastically.

'Why not? Find a rich guy. Fall in love. Just like your brother said.'

'I would rather turn . . . you know lesbian . . . and let you pay for me.' They giggled.

'You will find a guy, Shruti. Nice one. Rich one. It is the best career option you see. Better than Silverman.'

'Why don't you?'

'I don't want a rich guy. My father takes care of the rich part. To be frank . . . I don't want them at all.'

'Why don't you?'

'I just don't trust them. I know you might have heard it before. But still . . .'

'Hmm . . . find a poor, nice guy. I think I will settle for a rich one.' They both laughed.

'Rich one for you,' Garima said.

'Nice guy for you,' Shruti said and they laughed again.

Garima ended up buying the first of girly stuff for herself in years. And she admitted that she liked what she had bought.

# Their First Extravagance—Getting Drunk

As if Silverman wasn't enough, they were making it tougher for themselves. It had been a week and a half since the announcement and every one tried harder.

Classes were longer now. They all wanted to stick around. Everybody concentrated. Everybody asked questions. Everybody was back in their college frame of mind.

They were giving it their all. Notes were taken and filed. Coffee was gulped in ridiculous amounts. Water was splashed on faces at every break.

They were exhausted. Many of them skipped breakfast and morning bath just to get a few extra minutes of sleep. Tea breaks were replaced by short naps. A few of them puked and felt dizzy but it didn't matter.

'Want coffee?' Saurav asked Abhi, who was going through his notes.

'No. You go ahead.'

'C'mon Abhi. You can take a break.'

'I can't. I have to read this.'

'Five minutes won't make a difference.'

'It might. I don't want to get into more trouble.'

'I know that. Even I don't.'

'Not as much as I do.'

'Whatever.' Saurav looked away.

'Okay . . . I will come.'

'Nice.'

'Five minutes.'

'Five minutes only,' Saurav said. 'By the way, first salary today. Want to celebrate?'

'Talk about it later.'

They were back just before the lecture started. Everyone sat with the bottom of their spines touching the back of the chair. Nobody dared to blink or look at their watches or cell phones as the Wharton educated, Ermenegildo *Zegna* suited man, talked something about enterprise value and comparatives analysis in his heavy American accent. He took breaks to tell them how he rose in the company to become its Managing Director.

*Managing Director*

He was hardly forty and looked younger than most of the people working outside.

'I know it gets tough here. However, you will get used to it. Let me tell you, this is the honeymoon period. You can either make money or lose it. Right now you are expected to do none. So you can enjoy yourselves. I know it's a stupid thing to say to you when you work eighteen hours a day. But this is the reality of investment banking!' he said and smiled, quite sympathetically.

It had been eight months since Thapar had shifted from the US office to India to head the department and people had mixed feelings for him.

'The more we work the more credit he gets.'

Thapar gave the US office everything they wanted. People were working late hours, weekends, Sundays and national holidays. They were getting paid for it. And they were free to leave the company anytime they wanted to. It was fair.

Thapar was a sweet talker. It was hard to dislike him, even harder to argue with him. He was a godfather for the young people, a friend for the people of the same age and people older were either in awe or in envy. He was there to stay. I never liked him, though. I don't like men who are better than me. Especially if they have the hots for a girl named Avantika. You will know who she is in due course of time.

He continued the lecture and now questions poured aplenty. Every time a question was asked Saurav gave Abhi a disgusted look. That was because Abhi was always busy writing everything down.

The girls were trying desperately to get his attention. By now they had noticed that Thapar was undeniably charming. Peppered hair, chiselled features, a pointed nose and a tanned European complexion, not to mention, immaculately dressed.

Reminiscent of Daniel Ocean.

Thapar left. And left everyone behind, discussing him.

'What did she say?'

'Excuse me?' Abhi said.

Abhi and Saurav were again called up by Sumita for some disciplinary issue.

'I could have killed her,' Saurav butted in, banging his fist in his palm.

'That bad?'

'Very bad.' Abhi said.

'She is a bitch.'

'Shut up. He is here,' Garima said as she opened her notebook.

The trainer for the day was from the IT department and was there to make the joinees familiar with the various information security issues.

'Do you think he heard us?' Garima asked.

Abhi had not been able to take his eyes off her from the moment she came and sat next to them. She always sat in the opposite corner. All he had seen of her were her curly tar black hair and the indifferent look in her eyes.

'I don't think he cares. Probably he agrees.' Abhi said.

The class started and the IT guy started stressing on the importance of passwords and other related topics. All mails are tracked; they were told, inviting a scorn from many.

They were relieved when he said the class would end early. Nobody showed but every one of them envied the jobs they once looked down upon. They envied their friends who were back home by seven every day, while they slogged till two at night.

Nobody said it. They had heard stories of how speaking against the firm often results in unpleasant things. Sumita took special care of them.

The class went on and everyone kept fighting to keep their eyes from closing shut and heads from paining.

*Movie today? Ask her too. If you can.*

Saurav wrote on his pad and passed it on to Abhi. Garima peeked in.

| | |
|---|---|
| Abhi : | *Movie today? Salary celebration?* |
| Garima : | *You will not get the tickets. BTW, Which movie?* |
| Saurav : | *Any. Wolverine? New York? And why won't we get tickets?* |
| Garima : | *3 halls in Hyd. All seats are booked in advance. Don't even try.* |
| Saurav : | *Dinner?* |

Abhi : *Where?*

Garima : *Little Italy. Have heard about it. Free beer thrown in.*

Saurav : *I will ask other people. U ask the girls.*

Abhi : *hehehe.*

Saurav : *I was askin Garima.*

Abhi : *ohhh!*

Garima : *wot? I don't even know them.*

Saurav : *you don't even know us.*

Garima : *whatever. I will ask the girl from SRCC. She is sweet.*

Saurav : *and the girl from Presidency. Please?* ☹

Abhi : *hehehe.*

Garima : *Wot do I get?*

Saurav : *Chocolate.*

Garima : *Dark. And no nuts.*

Abhi : *hehehe.*

Saurav : *Shutup.*

Garima : *Shut up.*

Abhi : *Why? You need 2 concentrate on Information Security?*

Garima : *Bad joke.*

Saurav : *Terrible.*

Abhi : *Presidency? Bad choice.*

Garima : *Terrible.*

Saurav : *Abhi—Blind, Garima—Jealous.*

Abhi : *Shut up.*

Garima : *Shut up. I don't even know you.*

Abhi : *hehehe*

'What will you guys have?' Shruti asked as she had no clue as to what to order. Garima had asked Shruti and she was only too glad to join in.

'Not much of a drinker, Are you?' Saurav said as he poured over the menu card.

'Not at all. First time.'

'I will have a vodka. With lime,' Garima said.

'Never mind Shruti, even we don't drink. I have started very recently,' Abhi said.

'And you?' Garima asked Saurav.

'I have been drinking for quite some time now. But I never go overboard. Just beer. That too very occasionally. Anyway, Let us do it today. It will be fun.'

They called the waiter.

'A pitcher of beer. Abhi?' Saurav looked at Abhi for his approval.

'I don't think I will be able to finish it,' Abhi said.

'Make it two. I will help you guys,' Garima said.

'Oh . . . you drink?'

'And can hold it better than you,' she smirked.

The waiter came and Shruti bombed him with questions, much to the embarrassment of Abhi and Saurav.

*'How bad does it taste?'*

*'You will mix it?'*

*'Lime cordial? What is that?'*

*'Will it make us puke?'*

*'Don't get us too much.'*

The waiter could barely keep from laughing.

Salsa chips, Garlic bread platters with extra cheese; Chicken fresco and pastas were ordered.

Shruti and Garima promptly cut out the cheese and mayonnaise parts.

All of them had been geeks all their lives. They had been the only ones who even after the last exam of the year would go back to their rooms and match with a textbook whether their answers were correct. After every result they checked the margin by which they beat the person who came second.

And that day they lay sloshed outside an insanely expensive restaurant in uptown Hyderabad. It hit all of them except Garima, she being a big drinker unlike others, and it showed.

'You know what? I am going to run this place someday. Telling you dude. I will run this place. This sensex . . . this sensex, it's going up all because of me. And that bitch, Sumita, I will kill her. No seriously, I will kill her. Abhi will help me do that. My best friend. Don't think I am drunk. I am not. *Tu jaanta hai mujhe nahi chadti,*' Saurav said.

'*Haan, bhai. Abe saale*, if you run this company, what will I do? Let me run this company. You have four cars in your driveway anyway. And only nice girls like the two of you allowed. Will you work for me, you two beautiful ladies? May I have the pleasure of having you work under me?' He bent his head down till he fell over.

'Abhi. Abhi. Listen to me. Abhi. When are you asking Garima out? Tell me? She needs a nice guy like you!' Shruti asked out of the blue.

'Shut up,' Garima said, smoking her fifth cigarette that night. She sat there, not saying a word, smiling at people who were looking at the drunk trio.

'Why? Why should I? I am not nice. I am not even rich.

First I will get rich. Then I might just think about it.'

'But please do. She will be waiting. She likes nice guys.'

'And me? Whom do I ask out? I will also ask someone out. I think the Presidency girl was nice. Don't you think so?' Saurav said.

They spent an hour outside the restaurant before everyone was more or less sane and got into a cab. Abhi and Saurav reached Saurav's place after dropping the girls home.

Their bill for the night was fifteen thousand. And they were yet to start earning.

'You like her?' Saurav asked as he pushed the door open.

'Who?'

'Garima? Who else?'

'Why? Not really.'

'Why not? I think she is fine,' Saurav said.

'Why don't you ask her out?' Abhi asked.

'She is not my type.'

'What is your type? Fat? I am sorry . . . I didn't mean to . . . I wasn't referring to Megha . . .'

'It is fine even if you were . . . she *was* fat!' Saurav laughed. 'So, Garima?'

'What so? She is not my type either.'

'Elaborate.'

'She is very . . . you know . . . intimidating. She speaks less . . . those eyes . . . I mean she is nice looking but she is kind of . . .'

'Scary?'

'Yes. I mean you know . . . the rock girl types . . .'

'Those girls are awesome in bed.'

'Shut up Saurav.'

'So what are you going to do about it?'

'Nothing.'

'Nothing? Are you nuts?'

'I hardly know her. And besides, do you even think there is a slight chance that she would like anything in me?'

'She came out with us. She peeked in to what I wrote to you. And Shruti said something about you and her. Could be signs.'

'Could be.'

'Could be.'

They slept that day, after Abhi reminded him that they had an important training lesson the next day, not paying any heed to how much Saurav wanted to see the Presidency girl without her shirt.

That day, they finished their first month in Silverman.

# God Help Them. We Join The Class!

The office seemed a blur the next day. They all picked seats near each other; each one was holding his or her head, taking out time in between to look at each other with reddened eyes smiled.

The video of Saurav and Abhi dancing hand in hand was passed among the four of them and laughed at.

They all flopped down on the cafeteria couches as soon as they got their first break.

'Fifteen thousand?' Shruti said.

'Yes, without the cab fare. Add five hundred more to that,' Abhi added.

'That is a lot . . .'

'Don't worry . . . we will pool in . . . you can pay back as soon the next salary comes,' tapped on her shoulder and said.

Abhi looked at her and her eyes told him that she would explain it to him later. That was the time when Abhi realized, it was her eyes that drew him to her: big, black, screaming eyes that spoke a thousand words, in a blink.

'Thank you so much . . . I am so glad you guys called me,' Shruti said. She had gone through whatever happened a million times over last night. She finally thought she had a life, beyond parents, household chores and uninvited verbal and physical abuse.

'The pleasure is all mine,' Saurav said.

'Really? I brought her along. You wanted that Presidency girl. Didn't you?'

'Later,' he winked.

It was the last day of their month long training that was scheduled in the training room. After this day, the batch no longer would be together, but rather under their respective mentors, who were to help them in the initial stages of their career.

Saurav picked a seat near the Presidency girl, but their conversation lasted only a few minutes after which he came back to where he was sitting.

'What happened?' Shruti asked with concern in her voice.

'Nothing. She has a boyfriend. Been three years.'

'Sorry, Saurav,' Garima said.

'Why?'

'She doesn't have a boyfriend. I know her.'

'Maybe she lied to you.'

'Yes. Think. Who would she lie to, a harmless girl or a guy who is trying to hit on her. Tough choice, eh?'

'Bitch,' Saurav whispered.

Abhi's smile left his face abruptly as the familiar clicking clocking sound approached the door.

Sumita walked in a *saree* wrapped tightly around her two foot wide figure.

As if she wasn't any less menacing, she had chosen a bright red *saree*, smeared a lump of *kohl* around her eyes and a pancake of make up on her face.

'It seems like we finally have some well-dressed adults here.

Good.' She continued, 'Anyway, from Monday onwards, you will join you respective departments and mentors, who have been assigned to you according to how you performed during your training. The list has everything.'

As soon as she said this, every one flipped over the first page and started to look for their names.

Sumita banged the table and shouted out, 'And you *don't* have to look at it now. Not until I leave. For heaven's sake, don't act so childish! Anyway, all the mentors will come to you and will have a talk with you. We will leave you early today and you can spend some time with your mentors after all of them give you their presentations. You can ask them whatever you want to. You can take as much time as you want to. Carry on now.'

She left and everybody exchanged a beaten down look and sighed.

Abhi sank back to his chair as soon as he saw that Garima and he were in different departments.

Abhi and Shruti were put in Energy, Saurav and Garima got Infrastructure. The Thapar girls and the Sumita guys, those who sucked up to them, got M&A (Mergers and Acquisitions), supposedly the most glamorous department of SF.

The day started and so did the presentations. Every mentor had come prepared with an extensive presentation of how the company grew, how their departments grew and how they grew in the company.

Occasionally sprinkled with *how-good-I-am-and-was* anecdotes.

Group after group became disheartened for their mentors weren't what they had pictured them to be.

The guys were arrogant and tight ass, smart and hot nonetheless.

Nevertheless, it prepared the four of them well for their mentors, who were scheduled to be the last ones that day.

Quite surprisingly, the supposed mentor of Infrastructure didn't walk in. A guy walked in place of a female mentor and a silent *what-the-fuck* escaped Saurav mouth.

All eyes were now riveted on the guy. Not because he was insanely handsome, but because he was exactly the opposite. His hair was ruffled and fell over his eyebrows. It had been two days since he had shaved and there was bushy tuft of hair hanging from his chin.

A little bit on the heavier side, a rarity, shabbily dressed, another rarity, smiling too, catastrophic.

I could have gone further about the guy, but let us keep it short.

It was Deb. It was me. It was I (grammatically correct).

It had been six months that I had joined the firm and how and why of that will be answered in due time.

'The person you were expecting will be here shortly,' I said and pulled up my tie.

They weren't expecting me. They were expecting somebody with breasts. I was a huge disappointment.

'I guess she is here,'

She walked in.

This time everybody heard Saurav sigh and send air whooshing through his mouth. Guys who had slouched in their chair sat up straight and fixed their eyes on her. So did the girls. Their eyes had opened wide and mouths even wider. There was an uneasy silence in the room, no one moved, as they saw the most beautiful girl they had ever seen in their lives. Yeah, we are going out, so I am allowed to say these things about her. Not that they are very far from the truth either.

She looked at me and sent my heart aflutter as she always did.

'Hello, everyone. I am Avantika, Infrastructure.'

Avantika, the girl on whom every guy and a few females had their eyes on. Including Thapar.

She was beautiful. Great bright Angelina Jolie pink lips, a face cut along the right lines, very fair and the most beautiful eyes that could rob your soul and send you down a trip to heaven along the black hair cascading down her shoulders. As I always said, it was like a thousand light bulbs lit her face up. I am not saying this because it just happens that we are going out, but Avantika is the best looking girl you would ever see.

The guys were excited to bits on just the sight of her. Not that I blame them.

'Hi, I am Deb, Energy.'

I spoke, 'I am sorry but we have no presentation. I asked her to make one, but she spent hours taking a shower today morning. I, obviously, am totally incapable. Ishita and Ishaan must have told you everything you need to know about. If you didn't listen, never mind. It is of no consequence.'

Avantika butted in, 'See guys. This is a great opportunity for everyone. You know that. This job pays well. Yes, it is a little hectic . . .'

'A *little* hectic?' I interrupted.

'A lot. But we are being paid for it.'

'Paid? Ask them.' I have always been into office gossip and I knew about the internship programme.

'What? How can they do that?' Avanitka said after all the joinees shouted in unison about what Silverman did.

'They sure can.'

'Deb, how do you know?'

'How do you *not* know, Avantika? The *whole* office is talking about it!' I exclaimed.

'I have better things to do than talk to the whole office.'

I could have come up with something to answer to that, but she looked so cute that I couldn't think of anything witty.

'Anyway, class. Just six months. It is a little unfair, but this is what we have chosen to do. So, just stay here and be focused. You will be fine,' she said. She faked sincerity so brilliantly.

'You may lose your hair, have suicidal tendencies, and lose your boyfriends or girlfriends, if you have any. But yes, you will be fine,' I said.

I hated Silverman and made no bones about it. It had been more than once that I had run into trouble with Sumita.

'Don't say that. It isn't that bad.'

'It *is* and you know that.'

'Let them find out for themselves,' she said and rested the case. 'I don't think we have much to say here. But yes, we might not be all of yours' mentors but if you need anything, we will always be there. Feel free to ask. Anyway, what did Sumita schedule after this?'

'Time with mentors.'

'Hmmm . . . so who all are under us?'

Four of them raised their hands and Avantika asked them to meet her at the reception.

Shruti—Hot! Garima—Beautiful!

Lucky mentor I was.

It had been three years that Avantika and I had been together. I had joined the company a year after Avantika, after she had put in a good word for me in Thapar's ears. Thapar was head over heels over her and what he did not know then was that Avantika was dating me.

I had been a less than average engineering student at Delhi College Of Engineering. It made me an anomaly in Silverman Finance. I was almost universally hated in Silverman Finance. Firstly, because I joined the company very unceremoniously or through a jack, as they said. And secondly, I was dating the most beautiful girl in the company. And there was a third reason too, but no one really agrees with me on that—I am awesomely *good* looking.

Sumita especially hated me with all her heart, and would have seen me out of the company long back had I given her just one chance. She took it as her personal failure, having me in the company, she so zealously guarded against mediocrity. And people like me—mediocre.

Avantika was more like everybody else in Silverman Finance. She worked her ass off and tried to keep everyone happy and not just immediate seniors. But I kept her grounded, sane and emotionally alive, she had once said to me.

Just as we were leaving the office, we heard two female voices behind our back. Shruti and Garima were rushing towards us, while Saurav and Abhi followed them.

'Ma'am, we have this assignment to do. On the training we did. We have to submit it by Monday,' Shruti said.

'When did they start giving out assignments?' I asked.

'They have, this time. If only you would know something

more than office gossip,' Avantika said and smiled at the girls. 'So, you need help?'

'Yes, ma'am,' they echoed.

The guys reached us by then.

'Hmmm . . . but we are leaving for Pondicherry for the weekend. Just try doing it over the weekend by yourself and we will clear out your doubts on Monday, alright?'

'But ma'am, we have to submit it on Monday,' Abhi said.

'Hmmm . . . Okay. I have to leave. Deb sir will help you out, okay?'

'What okay? Where are you going?' I asked.

'I have to shop, Deb. There won't be any time tomorrow.'

'So? I am not missing the match for an assignment.'

'It is just a match.'

'It is the Delhi Daredevils.'

'Big deal.'

'And your shopping is?'

'We are leaving tomorrow. I have to.'

'So what?'

'Stop acting like a kid, Deb.'

'*You* stop acting like one. I am not missing the match. End of story.'

The four of them stood there watching us fight for another few minutes before Avantika said, 'Okay . . . I will take the girls along. You take the guys. We can do that, right?'

'Fine.'

'Fine.'

We stomped off and went our own ways.

Abhi and Saurav followed me outside the building, and we headed to the biggest screen in the whole of Hyderabad.

'Sir . . . this question . . . of the analysis . . .'

'Abhi . . . which department?'

'Sir . . . Energy.'

'Who else is in Energy?'

'Shruti.'

'Same assignment?'

'Yes sir.'

'Copy it.'

'What?' Abhi asked as if it was a sin to do so.

'And I do it from Garima?' Saurav asked, already slamming his laptop down.

'Just change the language. Make sure you do. You wouldn't want to get into trouble with Sumita . . .'

'Argh . . . !' we all shouted in unison as Delhi Daredevils lost another wicket.

'Terrible match . . . Rohit Kanojia should have hit that . . .'

'And if only Mathew had not wasted those balls . . .' Saurav added. The post innings discussion was on.

'Want to drink something?' I asked.

'I can . . .' Saurav said.

'Abhi?' I asked.

'Hmmm . . . okay.'

'Good for me . . . I anyway don't want to reach home before Avantika does.'

'Why?' they asked.

'Would have had to help her in the packing and stuff.'

'You live . . . together?' Abhi asked, a little scandalized.

'Half her wardrobe is there . . . so, yes, kind of.'

'That is so cool,' Saurav said.

'You bet it is,' I said as we clinked our glasses. 'So? What else about you two? Girlfriends?'

'No.'

'Nope.'

'Why not? Gay?'

'Waiting for the right girl,' Abhi said.

'I like the girl from Presidency. The brown haired one?'

'The one who wears black bras under white shirts?'

'You know her?'

'No. But it isn't that I am blind.'

'I tried asking her out. But she has a boyfriend, or so she says.'

'Okay. And Abhi, what are you looking for in your right girl?'

'I don't know.'

'He likes Garima.'

'You do? The girl with frizzy hair and brown eyes?'

'Yes, but I don't like her.'

'He thinks she is scary.'

'What? I thought she was pretty awesome looking.'

'I don't think she is scary. Just that she is too . . . you know . . . into herself . . . and she snaps back.'

'That way.'

Saurav added, 'In office she is okay, but otherwise, you know . . . she is all loose jeans, black nails, smoking and drinking.'

'So? We are drinking,' I said.

'Yes, we are, but she is a girl and Abhi gets intimidated by the fact. Even I do.'

'Tell me about it. Avantika was the same. She was an addict. But that was before I met her. I was petrified before meeting her, you know. Quite like you. Maybe more. I goofed up the first meeting, in possibly the worst manner. But things happened.'

'So what did you do?' Abhi said.

'Why do you want to know? I thought you didn't like Garima,' Saurav butted in.

'Nothing, really. In her case, all the things that she did were to hide herself from everybody, to run away. She is a very soft person otherwise. Luckily for me, I just found the soft person in her. Maybe it is different for Garima. Maybe not.'

'Maybe not.'

'Maybe not.'

We talked for a little while, had a glass of lime juice and headed home. Avantika still hadn't reached home.

'So, how does it look?' Avantika asked the two girls after she slipped into a micro mini. How could that possibly not look good!

'Very nice.'

'Nice.'

'Okay. So, we are done now? Garima, can you please check the list?'

'We are done.'

'Good. Let me change, till then see if you have any more questions to ask,' she changed and came out.

'No.'

'No.'

'Coffee?' she asked them.

'Sure.' they echoed.

They found cosy lounge chairs at the Café Coffee Day nearby and ordered their coffee.

'Will you girls have anything else?'

'No,'

'Can we smoke in here?'

'I am afraid not, Garima.'

'Hmmm . . .'

'You know what, Garima? You remind me of myself when I was your age. Younger, maybe.'

'Why?'

'I used to smoke. A lot. Weed. I have three tattoos of that time. Really crazy times. Experimented with a lot of things, you know.'

'So?'

'Why do you smoke?'

'I just like it.'

'No, there is some other reason.'

'There isn't any.'

'There always is. I smoked because it got me closer to my ex-boyfriend. He smoked because he thought it was cool. Later, he became an addict.'

'My smoking is not a problem.'

'She thinks that way she will not have to talk to people,' Shruti added.

'See? There is always a reason.'

'Whatever,' Garima looked away.

'Garima, I don't know you. Maybe I am all wrong. Have you heard of *Spirit of Living*?'

'Huh? The bearded guy?'

'Yes. I know you will be cynical. But just go to the convention once. Maybe it will help. I am not saying you need any. But it might just make your life a little easier. Shruti, you should go too.

'Okay, ma'am.'

'Just try it. There is nothing worse than running away from your fears. It leads to a road that never ends. Just try it.'

'I will see. Can we go now? I really need to smoke.' She got up and left the café to smoke outside.

# The First Taste

Shruti had promised to send everything beyond ten thousand home. When she told them about the internship programme, her dad shouted at her for being a selfish liar.

She had banged the phone down. Her mom called after that and told her how she would be responsible for her father's death, for the sorrow she caused him. She mailed them her internship letter the next day and cried the night out.

But things were a little different now. She had found a new lease of life. She could live out her dreams now. She never had friends earlier. She had now.

Shruti reached office at nine sharp. It was their first day in their respective departments.

She left with Abhi for the Energy department and started looking for me. They went to my desk, pulled up chairs and sat there.

'I am sorry, man,' I said loudly and immediately apologized to people around me as I panted. It was strange that on a floor where hundred people were working you could still hear an ant scream.

'Had a match. TT. Lost. But never mind . . . Sore ankle.'

'Good morning, sir,' they both said. I just looked at Shruti. She smelled good and looked fantabulous.

'Okay then, let us see, what seat have you been allotted?' I unlocked my computer.

Their seats were the fifth and the ninth seat from my cubicle.

I gave them their passwords to the computers and directed them to it.

'Sameer . . . your manager is still not here. When he comes, I will introduce you to him. Maybe then you can start working on something important.'

Abhi and Shruti reached their seats and logged in.

They received two mails from me as soon as they checked their inbox.

The first one said *best of luck.*

The second one had two attachments.

Pinball.exe.

Virtualtennis.exe

*Work hard.*

Meanwhile, Avantika had already assigned the other two some work. It wasn't anything important, but it was something that would help them in the days to come. They had to find some financial data and organize them in a usable way from data sources. *Google*!

Saurav was a little pissed off with the work assigned and asked Garima to help him out.

She snubbed him, but seeing him struggle with sleep in his eyes, she helped him out.

They were on their way to the cafeteria when I pulled them

away for something very important.

'I knew you would be here,' Avantika said as she stood at the door of the TT room.

'So?'

'What so? Your manager is here. And he is looking for you. And you two,' she said and looked at Shruti and Abhi, 'Rush to your floor. Saurav and Garima, that is for you too. And Deb, I need to talk to you.'

Avanitka waited for them to leave and then looked at me, visibly pissed.

'What happened?'

'What happened? Deb? What are these two doing since morning?'

'Nothing.'

'And why is that?'

'They just joined today. We can give them some time to relax.'

'We can't, Deb. They are not you.'

'What do you mean they are not me?'

'This job is important to them. You know the backgrounds of these two. It had been okay had it been Garima or Saurav, but don't do this to them. You can't play with their lives.'

'I am not. What . . .'

'Yes, you are. You didn't even help out with their assignments.'

'You are just getting worked up for no reason . . .'

'Don't act dumb. You know why I don't want you to screw things up. You know what Sumita wants from you. She made you a mentor because she wants you out of here. You are an eye sore to her. You slip with them and you are out of here. I will be alone here. And you will take those two down with you. If not for me, at least do it for them.'

She broke down. It wasn't the first time she had asked me to put my act together and act responsible. Seeing me leave the company would not be the prettiest sight for her. Neither for me.

'Good morning, sir.'

'Where were you?' Sameer asked scornfully.

'Downstairs.'

'Who won?' he winked.

Sameer was twenty-eight and an MBA from IIFT Calcutta. He wasn't very brilliant but was extremely hard working and terribly efficient.

Ever since I had helped to win over his wife of two years, we had been sort of friends. His wife and I were good friends. She often saw who was behind the cute surprises that Sameer occasionally sprang up.

I was spared some office work for doing that for him.

Abhi and Shruti were assigned work and they got busy. While the others worked, Abhi was a little distracted. He called up Saurav to ask whether he should call up Garima. He, quite obviously, said yes.

'Hi Garima,' Abhi said on the intercom.

'Hey.'

'What's up?'

'Working.'

'Nice. Too much work?'

'Not really.' She kept answering nonchalantly.

'What else?'

'I am sitting in my cubicle working. Nothing else.'

'Okay. Carry on. Sorry for disturbing.'

'Bye.' She kept down the phone.

Avantika, who was sitting right in the next cubicle, looked at her.

'*What?*' Garima said with her eyes and got back to her computer screen.

Garima was coming out from the smoking room, when Avantika happened to pass by.

'Any problems, Garima?'

'No ma'am,' she said as they both headed towards the lift.

No words were exchanged for the next few minutes.

'Ma'am.'

'Yes, Garima?'

'What do those conventions do?'

'Want to grab a coffee?' Avantika asked her and they headed for the pantry.

'Ma'am.'

'Call me Avantika. I feel like an old hag otherwise.'

'Avantika . . . I don't know why I am telling you this, but there is no one else . . .'

Garima went on to tell Avantika about Karan and something else that no one knew. Garima was abused as child, by her own uncle.

The memory of that hot day in May, five years ago gripped her and she recounted the incident to a shocked Avantika.

'I still remember every moment of it . . . He came to my

room . . . drunk . . . I can still feel his rough hands on me till this day . . . grabbing me . . . my own uncle . . . I could just scream in silence . . . I wanted to die . . . I so wanted to die . . . he kept violating me . . . I had grown up in front of him . . . and he . . . I punched him in the face and ran . . . After that day . . . I lay in the shower for hours every day and hoped the tears and the water would wash it away. It never happened . . . Karan had come to my rescue then . . . but when that ended . . . *everything* ended for me . . . Since then, I have been running . . . from people . . . from relationships . . . I don't want to be alone . . . but I am too afraid . . .'

Tears came streaking down. Avantika hugged her and patted her.

'Before Deb . . . my boyfriend asked me to please a friend of his . . . *forced* is the right word, not *asked* . . . In front of the whole section . . .' Avantika said.

'Then . . .?'

'I became you.'

'And?'

'I just stopped one day. The conventions helped, but it is you who has to fight. I fought. And things have never been better . . . I have Deb. I can't say he is the best guy in the world. But he is the best for me. He loves me. And I love him. I never would have got him had I not trusted him. Had I not taken the chance . . . You are a nice girl Garima, I know that. You have been through a lot, I know that too. Somewhere down the line, good things will happen to you. But that is only if you let them happen . . . Just let go of the past. There is a whole lifetime to live . . . don't lose out on that . . . Life has been unfair to you . . . to me . . . that is why we have all the more reason to make the rest of the lives wonderful . . .'

'Hmmm . . .'

'Shall we go?'

'Yes.'

'Let me see that smile first.'

Garima smiled.

'And black doesn't suit you Garima. Whoever told you that must be blind. Wear pink. We are girls, after all!'

They giggled and went to their floor.

Just as they sat on their seat, Garima looked at Avantika and moved her lips.

'Thank you.'

Avantika smiled.

Garima picked up the phone and dialled Abhi's extension.

'Hi Abhi.'

'Yes.'

'What yes? Garima, this side.'

'Oh, yes. Tell me.'

'I am sorry for the last time. Was a little rude. But was kind of stuck in some work . . .'

'It is okay . . .'

'What are we doing tonight?'

'We?'

'The four of us?'

Avantika, who was listening to conversation, smiled.

They talked for another fifteen minutes and made a plan to leave the office at sharp eleven and have dinner someplace. Saurav and Shruti were only too glad to agree. Saurav suggested a roadside *dhaba* and the plan was finalized, the first of many to come during that month.

# Love Brews

Weeks passed and they were hardly seen in office beyond the mandatory eleven o' clock.

No matter what happened, they pooled in all their energy in the last few hours to finish the allotted work of whoever was left behind. By Silverman standards, a thirteen-hour day was pretty relaxed. September went past without any hiccups.

The dinner at the *dhaba* near Banjara Hills was never missed, the high point of the day. Every day they dug in piping hot *paranthas* served with pickle and *dahi, at* the only place in Hyderabad where you could get authentic Punjabi fare. The dinners out in the open, on the rickety chairs brought them out of the monotony that Silverman offered them. That one hour that they spent every day at the *dhaba* made it all seem bearable. It made them feel alive. It made them pull through another day.

Friends do make the journey worthwhile.

Sundays were spent at Saurav's place, as none of them wanted to waste time travelling around in the hot sun. Movies were watched. Popcorns were popped. Beers were clinked, and they still drank like novices. Somebody or the other puked. Those three had started mounting pressure on Garima to stop smoking and it showed results. She was down to just a cigarette or two a day. Her clothes got an occasional dash of blue or green those days. So did the nails. She spoke a lot more now.

Sundays were spent as Sundays should be. Lazily. They called Avantika and me over once, and it was heartening to see four good friends putting everything behind them and getting on with life.

Staying together and trying to make something more of their lives just than what Silverman had to offer.

Abhi and Shruti's reason for staying at Silverman had not changed in the last two months, but Garima and Saurav's had.

'I can't leave them.' They both had said once. Adversity makes the best of friends. It had been two months that they had been together, but their bonhomie was unmatched. Their lives were wretched, but one thought of hanging out together wiped it all away.

'Hey, Abhi. What are you doing?' I asked.

'I was just sending you the profiles, sir . . . it will just take five more—'

'Leave all that. What about Garima?'

'What, sir?'

'What *what*? When are you asking her out?'

'I don't know, sir.'

'See, if you think I am a fool, I am not, Saurav told me all about it. Why didn't you tell me?'

'Sir . . .'

'Never mind . . . So when?'

'I don't know, sir.'

'Look Abhi . . . I am twenty three, you are just nineteen. So, there are a few things that I know better than you. When you get a girl as smashing as Garima, you don't let go. You understand? Especially if that girl likes you too.'

'What?'

'Hmmm . . . I am not lying, Abhi. Avantika told me this morning. And it is true. So just go ahead. Ask her out. She won't say no.'

'I will try, sir.'

'Good. And whatever you do, don't let anyone know that I told you this. Right?'

'Right sir.'

I walked away. If I would have had eyes in the back of my head, I would have seen him dancing his legs off.

For Garima, it was a new lease of life.

'I am so happy to see you smiling,' Avantika said.

Garima and Avantika went to *Spirit of Living* conventions whenever they got time.

'It is all because of them. I now wish I could go back to college and relive the moments . . . instead of sitting alone in the hostel and brooding . . .'

'Never mind, Garima. There is a whole lifetime left.'

'Hmm . . . I am so glad, I found them . . . . I feel so lucky and when I am with them . . . it is like . . . nothing ever happened . . . And I wouldn't have tried had it not been for you . . . Thank you, Avantika.'

'C'mon. Leave all that. Did Abhi say something?' Avantika asked.

'Naah. I don't think he will.'

'Why don't *you* say something? You like him, don't you?'

'I mean, he is very sweet . . .' Her cheeks flushed. 'Yeah, yeah. I like him. But I am not going to say anything . . . Are you sure he likes me?'

'Yes. Deb told me so.'

'Okay.'

'But don't tell anyone I told you, right?'

'Right.'

'What got you so late today?' Saurav asked. Shruti had stayed late that day in office. She had asked the other three to leave but Saurav stayed back.

'Nothing.'

'You cancelled today because of nothing?' Saurav joked.

'Yes.'

'Are you serious?'

'Yes.'

'Why?'

'Saurav, I can't come every day . . . I need to be here . . .'

'What are you talking about?'

'I just . . . I am just a little . . . I am scared, Saurav.'

'*Scared?* Why?'

'I don't want to lose this job.'

'You won't. You work hard. Why would you?'

'I don't know . . . '

'Why are you getting so negative about it?'

'Saurav, we are the only ones who leave the office so early. Have you seen anybody else do that?'

'But we complete our work. What is the point in staying back?'

'I don't know. I just think we should stay here a little more. Everyone completes his or her work, but they still stay here, just to show others that they are sincere.'

'So?'

'I am thinking of doing the same.'

'I think it is a silly thing to do.'

'I know . . . But even if it helps a little . . . I don't want to go back . . .' she said, her eyes moist.

'You won't have to.'

'I am sorry, Saurav.'

'I understand Shruti.'

'Thank you.'

'And I know they won't fire you. Just in case they even think of getting rid of you, don't worry. My father has some connections. He will get you a job. Trust me.'

'*Pakka?*'

'Cross my heart and hope to die.'

'Thank you.'

'The pleasure is all mine.'

'So, what's with Anamika?'

Anamika was another colleague of theirs whom Saurav had been trying to hit on since many days.

'Nothing . . . She says she wants to concentrate on her career and doesn't have time for all this. What bullshit!'

'That is sad. Isn't that the fifth girl you have asked out here?'

'Shut up! Why don't *you* be my girlfriend?'

'Yes, why not? We all know what you want in your girlfriend. A couple of months of fun and then you will dump me. Sorry Saurav. Look someplace else.'

'Hmmm . . .' He made a sad face and Shruti pulled his cheeks into a smile.

'You will find someone. Who is hot and . . . good in bed . . . and who doesn't mind breaking up . . .'

They both laughed.

'Better than you?'

'Better than me,' Shruti said. 'Where are they?'

'Garima's place, I think.'

'Would something happen?'

'Let's hope so.'

'Yes. He is the kind of the guy she wanted.'

'What kind of guy do you want?'

'Rich guy.'

They laughed.

'You really loved her, didn't you?' Garima asked Abhi.

'Yes, sort of. I mean she was all I thought about then. She was the only real friend I had.' He sighed and looked out at a distance from the veranda they were sitting in. 'You tell me, never thought of going back to him?' he asked.

'Million times.'

'Why didn't you?'

'It was easy going back. It was difficult staying away. Never mind, I am almost over it.' She looked away.

'I am sorry I asked,' he said and stood close to her.

'It is okay. There used to be a day when even thinking about him made me cry. But no longer.' She clutched his arm. It sent tingles down her spine.

'Goo . . . good . . . Ummm . . . to hear that . . . Listen . . . there is something I have been meaning to tell you.' He looked into her eyes.

'Go on.' She stared back.

'You . . . have . . . beautiful eyes . . . '

'Thanks.'

'And . . .'

The harder she stared at him, the greater tingles she got, the more he stuttered.

'Should . . . we go . . . and yo . . . you . . . kn . . . know . . . eat something?'

'Yes, sure.' She let go of his hand and cursed him from within.

The last day of their second month, the four of them partied the whole night away, despite earnest requests from Shruti to keep from doing so.

'What happened yesterday?' Saurav shouted. His voice was barely audible over the roaring speakers of the nightclub.

'Nothing,' Garima said.

'Nothing?' Saurav shouted.

They both entered the common washroom.

'He didn't say it. I think he was about to. But he didn't.'

'Did you touch him? Hold his hand? Or something?' he nudged.

'Yes, why?'

'He gets nervous. Next time, don't do it.'

'Thanks for the tip,' she said as she darkened her lipstick.

'You have changed.'

'In a good way?'

'You look beautiful now.'

She was wearing a silver halter that night. Far cry from the kind of clothes she used to.

'Thanks, Saurav.'

'You look like a girl.'

'Thanks again.'

'It is strange, though.'

'What is?'

'Everybody knows that you guys love each other. You know that he likes you. He knows that you like him . . . but . . .'

'Wait . . . wait . . . wait . . . What? He knows?'

'Obviously, he knows.'

'Who told him?'

'Deb.'

'But . . .'

'As if . . . didn't Shruti and Avantika tell you that Abhi likes you?'

'But does he know that I know that he knows?'

'Whatever.' Saurav went off to pee.

The next day, they all reached office with a huge hangover.

# They Get Screwed . . . Amongst Others In The Parking Lots

Garima and Saurav reached office that day to find Avantika and Dinesh standing on their seats.

Dinesh was their manager and Avantika's boss.

'I think and I know that you will be able to work on a deliverable,' he said matter-of-factly. Dinesh had joined the company a few years back and didn't enjoy a very good rapport with people below him. He was known to give girls a harder time than guys.

'But sir, don't you think we should practice a little more before that,' Saurav butted in.

'No,' he said. 'I have given a list of ten companies to Avantika. Take them from her. I want the profiles by this night. Avantika, you run a quality check on it and then we will send it by tomorrow. Clear?' he asked.

They answered in the affirmative. Avantika nodded and walked away.

Saurav and Garima heard her mutter *bastard* under her breath. They looked at her with blank faces. They didn't know what to make of it.

Avantika went to her seat and mailed them the data source

and the company names.

Lecherous bastard. If I had it my way I would have pushed a rod through his heart for the way he looked at Avantika.

It was ten in the morning then.

Shruti and Abhi called them for lunch. They waited till two and then ate without them.

After lunch, Sameer was called up by Sumita and asked to give details of whatever Abhi and Shruti had been doing. She had the swipe in times with her, along with the time spent by us in the TT room.

Sameer was given a solid pasting on being irresponsible and unprofessional with the joinees under him. Sumita humiliated him and said not-so-kind things about him and me. She threatened him with consequences which were not too nice to hear. With increments in sight and recession on the horizon, such meetings were the nightmare of many. Sameer somehow pulled through the harsh words and politely took Sumita's leave.

He sat down on his seat and leaned back and took a deep breath.

I let Sameer know that I had assigned work to them. And also that Sumita was a bloody whore and he should not mind whatever she said.

We had a small talk and went back to our work in a few minutes.

It was six in the evening and all four of them were working. That didn't change until twelve in the night.

The clock struck one. Saurav was waiting for Garima to finish off the work when Dinesh approached Saurav.

'Done with what I had asked you to do?'

'Almost, sir. Just one hour.'

'Have you checked the format? This is the wrong one,' Dinesh said as he peered at his computer screen.

'Sir . . .'

'At least read the guidelines properly. You even had a training lecture on that one. You have read those, haven't you?'

'No . . . sir . . . guidelines?'

'Then how come you are working? I hope you know there is a certain format that every document is presented in. Without it, everything that you do is a waste. I don't know what you were doing during the lectures. Anyway, you know where they are kept?' Dinesh asked, half disgusted, half irritated.

'Sir . . .'

'Go and ask Avantika. Go through them today. It is not much. 80 odd pages. Go through that and I will mail you some work that has just come up. This is an extremely urgent deliverable and I need it tomorrow morning. I need both, you and Garima to start working on this.'

'But sir . . . '

'Is there any problem?'

'No Sir.'

'Good.'

Dinesh walked away.

It took Saurav and Garima four hours to complete it.

They left the office at five in the morning. Life had started to suck. Big time.

October was traditionally the most hectic month for Silverman before the lull of November and December and it was proving to be so. Days were getting hectic each passing day. No one slept for more than four hours a day.

Things had worsened. They were just starting out and the only help they got was from us—Avantika and me. Others on the floor had no interest in wasting their time on them. Dinesh was way too condescending to approach. Sameer was better, but he was overworked too.

Garima and Shruti had started getting dark circles and they too had gone the Silverman way. Dollops of foundation to hide it. Saurav and Abhi had stopped to take showers to get that extra sleep time.

There was a constant look of sadness and depression on their faces from the lack of sleep and the stress that came with it. It was withering them away. The fun Sundays were over. They were now spent sleeping in their respective flats.

Saurav had thought of resigning more than once, but Garima had begged him not to. She would be alone in the department and that was the last thing she wanted.

'Go to the cafeteria and sleep. Give me your password and I will complete it,' Garima said that day. Saurav had been dozing off in office.

'What if Dinesh—?'

'I will manage,' she cut him off.

Saurav nodded and walked away in a daze without realizing that enormity of the favour that she had just extended to him.

Saurav had been pushed into working out by the other three and that meant another hour of sleep gone. He was sceptical at first. It was when they told him that the flab was the reason why he wasn't getting any girls, he agreed.

Saurav went to the couch and fell asleep in a matter in seconds.

Two hours later, at around three in the night, Garima went to the cafeteria and woke him up from his slumber. They left.

They took the way that went through the parking lot. Saurav's idea. He always looked for new cars that kept adding to the burgeoning SF parking lot. Garima was waiting at the opening gate of the parking while Saurav went around the cars in eights to get a full view of the cars.

It had been five minutes when Garima looked back to see no sign of him. He must have crouched to have a look at some customized alloy wheels, she thought.

She waited for another two minutes after which she got a little worried and called him up. His phone was unreachable. She headed for the parking lot.

She walked inside the lanes of the dimly lit parking lot, lined with dark cars all along. She was scared now. The darkness was eerie. A light flickered and her heart skipped a beat. The clocking of her heels echoed in the parking lot. She was sweating at the brow now as she passed a few more cars and saw no sign of anyone there. She took out her cell phone. No network.

Garima contemplated running out of there but she feared something had happened to Saurav down there. She kept walking, taking measured steps and looking everywhere, clutching her handbag close to her body. She felt somebody looking at her from the darkness. Somebody following her. All the time. She stopped more than once to look around only to hear shifting steps and the sound of her heels on the floor. She walked into the darkness, further away from the exit. Her steps got smaller. Her breath heavier. Darkness engulfed her. She reached out for her cell phone again, as she felt an urge to run.

Just as she crossed a black Tavera SUV, she heard feet shifting across the floor behind her. All of a sudden she felt hands crushing against her stomach and face and pulling her down.

She blacked out as the hand gripped tightly against her face and pulled her behind the car. The man pinned her to ground.

She kept struggling and kicking. Her head banged against the door of the SUV, as she kept swinging her head wildly at Saurav, who had blood in his eyes.

'What? What? What the . . .' she shouted, still half struggling while her face was covered with Saurav's hand.

'Let me explain. I am trying to rape you. Stay down and it will be over.'

Her eyes were teary and shouted a *why* at him.

She had frozen. Her eyes were now bloodshot and were quivering.

He came close to her ear and she closed her eyes as tears came down.

'I can't believe you fell for that!' he whispered out loud and smiled at her.

He let her loose.

She cried out and rained blows on him while he ducked and swayed out of her reach. He muffled her again.

'Stop it. Stop it. They will know we are here.'

She bobbed her head vigorously and he left her.

She whispered, 'You will pay for this. You could have killed me, for heaven's sake.' She punched him. 'And why are we hiding like this? And who are *they*?' she whispered.

'You will see.'

A familiar face entered the car park from the lobby, looked all around himself for some car. He checked the keys in his hand and the number plates of the cars.

He walked on passing the car they were standing behind. He kept inspecting the cars till he stopped near an off white Honda Captiva. The door was open. He looked around and entered the car. And banged the door shut.

The man was Rajat Thapar.

'Why isn't he driving?' Garima said in a hushed tone.

'Because it is not his car.'

'What?'

'Shut up.'

Saurav held her hand as they crept up to the car next to the white SUV. It wasn't the best view they could have got but Garima could make out what Saurav wanted to show her.

She could recognize her hair anywhere.

'What the . . .' Garima almost said out loud. 'That girl is *Anamika*? What the hell is she doing with Thapar? What the hell is going on here?'

'How am I supposed to know? Seems like this is her idea of concentrating on her career.'

'Shit.'

'Were you following her?'

'No comments . . .' he whispered. 'I thought she is a lesbian and had come here for Kiran.'

'Kiran?' he asked, with eyes so wide, one could have grabbed her contacts out of them.

'She is in there too.'

'You are not doing that,' Garima said as soon as Saurav fished out his cell phone.

'Yes, I am.' He pushed her back and crept a few steps further till he reached the back windshield of the car. He kept low and raised his hand till the cell phone screen showed all three of them.

What they saw, and later we saw in video is something we would never forget.

Thapar ran his fingers though the girl's hair as he kissed her. He started to assault Anamika's neck as his hands slipped down to her shirt. He unbuttoned it slowly and took it off. He pushed something and the seat flattened to a bed. The girl climbed on to Thapar, pulled her skirt up a little, unhooked her bra and it came off. It was stripped off by Kiran. Kiran was a year senior to her, whom they had earlier missed seeing in the car. While Thapar and Anamika kissed, Kiran had unzipped Thapar's pants and pulled them down. Kiran got naked and helped Anamika to get out of the skirt she wore. They both started working on Thapar as if he had taken a dip in a chocolate fountain, while Thapar egged them and grabbed their shapely parts now and then. Anamika had possibly the most gifted rack in Silverman and Thapar made the most of it. Thapar took turns with them, moaning like a boar, as the car shook and fogged up. Spent, they lay there, Thapar and the two girls, naked and kissing.

Saurav had got up in between to see what was happening, and he sat down again, his mouth frothing, after seeing what was going on.

They rushed out of the parking lot as soon as Garima heard the door lock click.

'Can you believe it?' she clutched his hand and asked.

'Anamika. That bitch. *Concentrate on career*? I told you then, it is all bullshit.'

'Did that really happen?'

'It did.'

'I mean how? How? And . . . why? What on earth was that?'

'I am as clueless as you are.'

'Show me the video,' she grabbed his cell phone.

Within the first few minutes, she handed it back to him.

'Did you see them? Bloody nymphets. That bitch Anamika.'

'What? The way I see it. It is Thapar. These girls wouldn't have offered themselves. Bloody pervert, he would have asked for it. And you . . . chauvinist . . .'

'Yeah . . . okay.'

'Is there anything we can do about it?'

'Hmmm . . . I don't think so. Not at the risk of screwing our career and the girls' lives.'

'I never thought . . .'

'Me too.'

'I mean . . . *Anamika*? She came here with us.' She held her head.

'I know.'

'This is so unfair . . . and sick.'

'Hmmm.'

'Can't we do something . . .? Anything?'

'Nothing that won't involve a police case. And you wouldn't want to get involved.'

'Hmmm . . . '

'But still . . . something, Saurav?'

'I don't think so.'

Garima started to shiver and stagger. Her eyes were rolling and it looked like she would faint.

'Are you okay?'

'Yes . . . I am fine . . .'

Saurav helped her into the cab.

'Are you going to be okay? Or do I—?'

'I am fine.'

'Okay.'

'Bye.'

'Bye . . . and by the way . . . '

'Yes?'

'The car was Dinesh's.' Saurav said.

The cab drove off.

She got down and walked up to her apartment. She was tired and her head was still spinning.

The joke that Saurav played on her in parking lot brought back the most painful of her memories. The helplessness of girls, the groping of Saurav . . . she didn't feel too nice.

Her phone beeped.

*Goodnight. Sleep well.*

*Abhi.*

She called Abhi up. She had just started narrating the parking lot incident, when Abhi told her that Saurav already told him. He sensed that she was crying. He asked her to go to sleep but she could not.

She was on the phone for an hour, silently sobbing while Abhi kept holding on the other side. It was one of those nights when the thoughts of those two days of her life clouded her mind and she didn't feel nice about anything.

After she told him about what she had told Avantika that day, it took an hour for Abhi to book a cab and get there.

'Will you have something?' Garima asked him.

'Have you had anything?' he looked at her and asked. She was in a better mood now.

'Yes. I mean . . . No.'

'Never mind. I will make you something good to eat.'

'You can cook?'

'Of course I can cook. I used to cook a lot in my college days,' he said, acting shocked.

'So what are you making for me today, chef?'

'It is a very easy thing to make. But it is tastes like heaven,' he said as he rummaged through her kitchen. 'It is probably French but I make an Indian version. Spicy. Works well with ketchup. Just wait.'

'So, what is it?'

'You might have heard about it. It is very popularly known as *Maggi.*'

'Argh . . .!' she said out loud and started to hit him playfully. They got into a cute little mock fight which ended when they both felt a little something going down their spines, whenever they touched each other.

They parted.

'Okay, I will sit here,' she said and climbed up the slab, right next to the stove.

He proceeded to crush the cakes into small pieces and added them to the steaming water. All this time, Garima sat there, looking at him as he did very carefully what people could do with their eyes closed.

'You are sweet.'

'I know,' he said as he rolled a noodle around a fork and made her eat it.

He made her finish the Maggi and found an apple in the fridge for her to eat. After that, he put her to sleep.

As soon as he left the bedroom and opened the main gate to leave, she said, 'Please stay . . .'

'But . . .'

'Sorry . . . you can go . . .'

'I will stay.' He bolted the door.

He hugged her. Her eyes were a little moist.

'Thanks for staying.' Garima clutched his hand and kept her head on his shoulder.

'I wanted to stay.'

She smiled. She grabbed his hand and put it across her shoulder and asked him, 'Is there anything that you wanted to say?'

'What? Me? No . . . I don't think so,' he said, shocked.

'Saurav told me.'

'What . . . what? What did he tell you?'

'That . . . you know . . . that you like me.'

'He is such a . . .'

'You didn't want me to know?'

'No . . . I did.'

'So?'

'It would have been better had I told you.'

'And when were you planning to?'

'Today!'

'So?'

'You are the best thing that has ever happened to me, Garima.'

'Go on.'

'I don't know what to say.'

'Then find something to say.'

'I don't know, Garima. The thing is, I really like you. I don't know what to call this, but what we have is so . . . complete. It feels so right. Perfect. To be with you. To be around you. It all comes so naturally to me. I mean, I really love you Garima. I really do . . . I really want you around . . . like forever . . .'

'See? You found something.'

'Not really the response I was looking for.'

'Aww . . . I love you too.' She pulled him near and pecked him.

'Thank you . . . but not really the kiss I was looking for either,' he smirked.

'Is it so . . .?' she smirked back.

She bent over and he pulled her over him. Her lips touched his and they kissed, exploring each other as if to make up for all the time they hadn't kissed. His hands ran through her fuzzy hair, her flawless skin. She grabbed his hair and pulled at them. The kiss lasted an eternity.

It ended with a stare into each other eyes. Many more small kisses followed thereafter. Abhi was hooked to her honey sweet lips.

Abhi pumped his fist and said, 'First kiss.'

'How mean!'

'You should be happy it is with you.'

'With Riya?'

'That was just a peck and it was just because I had done her assignment once.'

'Okay. And it wasn't bad for the first time. Come here. Let's try it again,' she said.

They kissed again.

The mention of Riya and first kiss brought back memories for both of them. Memories they would rather forget.

They spent the day in each other's arms thinking that this would be a new beginning.

# Of Fired People and Broken Windshields

'Yes, Thapar,' Sumita said as she entered his room.

'Things are looking down,' he said. Thapar's tone never showed the urgency of any situation, breezing through entire life changing discussions as if deciding what to eat for lunch.

'I heard. Did they call?'

'Yes. The subprime thing has really started to hit. Too early to say, but pundits fear the worst.'

'What is the worst?'

'We are looking at halving the workforce.'

'Are you serious?' Sumita was sweating now. She pulled up a chair to sit.

'Yes. Probably me. And you too.'

'What? Why me?'

'Extra staff.'

'What do you mean? I have upheld the values of the firm for so long. They can't do that to me. I am . . . I am the Head HR.' For probably the first time Sumita had gone soft.

'Don't worry yet Sumita. There is still time. And do something.'

'When should I start worrying?'

'Pretty soon. If we don't show them performance, we are cooked.'

'What? Half the staff is working nights.'

'Make it full then. I don't care. Show me some figures. I want the charts to go up. Bring up managers, threaten them with life. Make it work. I want man hours, quality man hours. And if that does not happen . . .'

'Then?'

'Anything can happen.'

*Earlier that month*

'Are you okay working nights?'

'Yes, sir, certainly.'

'The schedule may go into days.'

'I have no problem, sir. This is how I will learn. I am a very hard worker.' She gave him a disarming smile.

'Are you sure?'

'Yes sir.'

'You will be able to live alone? And the stipend is not much, you might know about that now.'

'Yes sir. But that won't be a problem. I can make friends quite easily, I am sure I will be able to manage it. Besides I have some friends in Hyderabad.'

'Oh, you do?'

'Yes sir.'

'And where do they work?'

'One of them works in this very company. Silverman Finance.

He was a great friend of mine . . . my senior, Abhi. I don't know if you know him . . . Tall, fair . . . wears spectacles . . . No, I guess he had started . . .'

'Okay, okay! I get it. Seems like it is time to meet that friend of yours. Welcome to Silverman Finance. You will get your formal acceptance for the internship in a while. Congratulations Riya.'

Jagdish, a known pervert had taken the interview. Riya had it easy. She just had to look good.

It had been six months that she had broken up with Arjun. More precisely, Arjun had dumped her, when Riya took a stand of not sleeping with him.

Since then, she had concentrated on her studies as she couldn't bear the sight or thought of Arjun anymore. That meant no more movies with friends. Or night outs. However, she still wore pink, slightly muted shades, though.

Not to mention, her new peer group in college—the geeks—got a makeover, thanks to her.

All the hard work had paid. She had bagged the coveted internship at Silverman Finance along with a few others. She was happy about that. Although she dreaded meeting Abhi again, she knew she had missed him.

Shruti was working hard. She was slogging her ass off. Everybody knew she desperately hung on to the job with all her life. She had not even once expressed displeasure at working so hard, having accepted it as her reality.

She always looked drained and no matter how hard I or her friends tried to get her off work, she was giving it her all.

Garima and Shruti spent the evening cursing Silverman

Finance and all their bosses and super bosses and sometimes the high salaries they drew.

Shruti had bought a pair of platinum earrings that evening. Her first extravagance.

Shruti had tagged along Garima to every jewellers shop in town before she got herself those earrings. By the end of the day, all Garima had for Shruti was a string of curses.

'Want to eat something?' Shruti asked Garima as they entered home.

'Obviously. I am starving.' Shruti whipped a parantha each and served.

'Not again,' Garima said.

Shruti was wearing those earrings again.

'Don't worry. I am not asking you again,' Shruti laughed. 'What is this?' she asked as she found a card while looking for a newspaper to put her plate on.

'Oh, that? Was just making a card for Abhi.'

'Why?'

'Generally.'

'Hmmm . . . nice . . .'

'It is such a good feeling, Shruti. To be in love. '

'Hmmm . . . I know . . .' Shruti said, half lost.

'Thinking of him?'

'Who?'

'Sachin.'

'Hmmm . . .'

'Don't worry, Shruti. You will find someone.'

'What if I want him?'

'Then, why don't you look for him?'

'I don't know . . . I don't know if he even wants me. And

somehow, I feel it was never meant to be. At least, we still loved each other when we parted . . . at least it is a good memory . . . and it will always be . . . he will always be . . .'

'Amen.'

'Hmmm . . .'

'C'mon. Now don't get all teary. You got yourself new earrings, right? And they look beautiful. And anyway, we will find you a guy . . . a rich dashing guy . . . someone who will get you new earrings every day . . . maybe even that pendant you so liked . . . right?'

'Right,' Shruti said, her eyes moist, but still smiling.

Just before the next day ended, the four of them checked their mails to find what every employee of the IBD division dreaded of. A meeting with Sumita Bhasin. It was sent to all four of them along with me, Avantika and their managers.

It spelt terror for them, disgust for me, worry for Avantika and *what the fuck* for the managers. For Saurav and Abhi, it was their third call up in three months! November had just started!

All seven of us waited outside her room, Dinesh being the only one who was breathing a little easy.

They were called in just as I went for a leak. Bad luck.

Everyone waited, along with Sumita, for me to return. I entered hurriedly and got the look from her.

Sumita was poring over some papers and the very next second, she almost slid them violently to Dinesh and Sameer, the only two who were sitting.

'Terrible,' she said.

'I know, ma'am,' Dinesh said. The papers were from the QC, the quality check department.

'So? What are you doing about it, Dinesh? Five mistakes on an average? And you, Sameer? No point saying anything to you. Three years and you still don't take anything seriously, do you?' She stood up.

'Let me make one thing very clear to you. Three years, five years or one. We are not here to cut any slack. You make mistakes, you leave. Do I make myself clear?' She looked at everybody. 'Deb? What will you do if you get fired? These guys may still manage something, but *you*? What will *you* do?' She paused and looked around before she continued, 'And everyone, one more report like this comes, and heads will roll. Now, get out every body, and I hope not to see your faces again. I hope I make myself clear.'

'And yes, we have made the shortlist of new joiners who would go to Singapore,' she said. I could see their faces turning red. 'And none of you are going. We are sending fifteen, you are in the other nine. Make sure the nine of you don't fall like nine pins!' She laughed out like only a witch would, voice shaking the very foundations of the office. She leant forward and stared into Shruti's eyes which were now red and little wet.

'Shruti, you came real close. I have no qualms telling you that you were better than the fifteen who are chosen. But the management thought otherwise . . . for the kind of company you keep . . .' She waved her hand around the other three. ' . . . is very disruptive for the company. You can still make amends. The list still needs to be signed by Thapar. Talk to me sometime. We will see what we can do. Thapar and I.' She leant back and motioned everyone to leave.

Shruti left the room crying.

I was the next one to leave the room after I let a Hindi expletive followed by a fuming Dinesh.

Tough times were ahead.

Sumita had something planned for Shruti for sure. Sumita and Thapar.

It had been three hours since Shruti hadn't been on her seat. She was in the cafeteria. Crying.

The three of them were pushing each other to go talk to her first. The pushing ended with Saurav going first to sit next to her. 'Hi, Shruti . . .'

The others came and joined them.

'I mean, we can stay away from you in the office if you want to,' Abhi said while she looked up, her kohl smeared with the crying.

'Shruti, we are really sorry,' Garima said.

Shruti looked at them, flicked a few strands of hair out of her eyes and said, 'You really don't get it? Do you? I am finished. I am not getting through this programme and neither are you. But how does it matter to you? Saurav, you are an IITian, you have nothing to fear. You will go back to Delhi to your big car and big house. Abhi and you can go back to your families, get a job and settle down. What am I supposed to do? Haan? You have any idea what I go through every day when I am there. I am locked up. I can't go out. I am made to work the hardest. You know what? I would have got married by now had I not got this job. They lie nowadays that I am at my grandmother's place. Why? The guy they selected for me doesn't want me to work. And now that I lose this, I have nothing left. The pan belching bastard . . . doesn't make a difference to my parents if he sleeps with a million prostitutes. You know why I am doing this job? My parents want the money so that they can stuff his filthy mouth with it. So that there is some chance that he doesn't hit me after I become his bed whore. So that he doesn't burn me with his cigarette after he finishes with beating me blue. You don't believe me he will do that? But you will, when you see his previous wife. Why? Why? Why my parents still want me to marry him? My father owes them crores. How so much? *I don't know.* But I know I am nothing more than a payment for them. I am nothing but a whore, a prostitute who they are selling to him. To get my father's sins paid. Are you still sorry?' She finished and left for the girls' washroom.

While Garima was crying, Abhi and Saurav had tears in the corners of their eyes.

All this time they knew about this, but the gravity of the situation hadn't hit them until now.

Sumita's outburst had everyone riled up, so while Shruti was in the cafeteria, I was working my ass off.

Little did I know what Sumita had planned for me the next day.

That night Sumita must have called Thapar to discuss a few things. Shruti and I being in those few things.

The next day, I found my termination letter on my table. It was not a surprise how and why it reached there. I had always expected it to come my way but still I was overwhelmed by anger and disgust when I saw that letter.

I stormed in to Thapar's room for had I gone to Sumita I would have knocked her down.

'What the hell is this?' I asked and sent the letter flying to Thapar.

'That is it, Deb. Rash behaviour. You are a negative influence.'

'What do you mean? I have everything in place, sir. I haven't fucking missed any target ever..'

'It is not about targets. Your style of working does not suit this office.'

'What bullshit is that?'

'See, this. Your language, the way you take things so lightly! It is even affecting the kids under you.'

'But they are doing well under me.'

'Not as well as the ones under Avantika.'

'But . . . sir. This is just not fair and you know that.'

'Deb, I have a meeting. You have to leave. Talk to Sumita if you need any clarifications. And further your manager had signed on your termination letter.'

I left. I knew it was of no use.

Sameer would have no choice but to sign on it. The manger's permission to fire anybody was just a sham.

Just as I was leaving, Thapar said to me, 'You are lucky, Deb. You have more time than others to look for a fresh beginning.'

'Whatever.'

I left and slammed the door behind me.

I called up Avantika and we met up in the cafeteria. Avantika chided me for being so rude to Thapar and screwing my case further. But then she kissed me and things seemed better. She assured me that we would be together, come what may.

I wasn't in the mood to talk to anyone else in the office before leaving.

Though I met the security guy on my way out, someone I was often involved in small talk. He was also someone who had his fill from the half empty vodka bottles that I gave him.

'I am sure that bastard did this,' Sumita said as she looked for any activity in the parking lot. There was none. For a few minutes, the security camera videos went off and came up again. In those few minutes, her brand new CRV windscreen was smashed and the word *bitch* was scratched over the bonnet.

'Where the fuck is the video? Give me that footage, you filthy rat,' she threatened Naresh, the head of security. There was lag of an hour of video.

'The video of that one hour goes to Thapar every day. He deletes them himself.' Naresh said.

'That bastard pervert! But how the hell did Deb know about this?'

'I don't know, ma'am.'

'Of course you know . . .' she said and stormed off.

There were a few dents and the rear tyres were punctured too which missed her eye the first time.

I felt a little peaceful after I trashed her car.

The prospect of not seeing Avanitka every day and seeing her lesser than usual saddened me.

That day I realized, the only reason why I was still there was Avanitka. She meant everything to me. I had always planned to marry her.

When she landed herself this overpaying job, I just got surer.

# Old Skeletons, Old Perverts

Days after I left the office, Riya had her first day in there, as a winter project intern.

She looked over her shoulder to spot Abhi but could not. She did not think he would talk to her anyway.

Saurav was hanging around the reception trying to see if something worth a try had turned up in this batch of youngsters.

Not surprisingly, she stood out in her shiny pointed heels, chunky glittery watch, streaked hair and undeniable good looks. Her smile was only too noticeable to miss. She lit up the place with her beamer. He asked a few people around and went nuts when he got to know that she was from SRCC.

He rushed to the cafeteria to ask Abhi if he knew her.

'Abhi!' Saurav called out from a distance.

'Yes?'

Saurav pulled him away from Garima and asked him. 'Do you, by any chance, know Riya? Your college junior?'

'Why? Why do you ask?'

Abhi didn't remember telling him about Riya and Garima for sure hadn't mentioned her either.

'She is downstairs.'

'What? What is she doing here? Did she ask about me?'

'And that means you know her?'

He, for a second, thought probably she had come all the way to apologize. But she had nothing to apologize for.

'Abhi? Do you know her?'

'Yes, but why? Did she say anything to you? Why is she here?'

'No. She is in the batch of new interns. Will you introduce me to her?'

'No.'

'Why? Not close enough.'

'No. We were friends . . . but . . . '

'Brilliant! Superb! Old friends . . . Please let's go downstairs,' Saurav said and started to pull him towards the lift.

'Please, Saurav . . . It is of no use. I will not talk to her. I don't want to. Please don't force me to,' he jerked his hand free and walked away leaving Saurav bewildered.

'What just happened between the two of you?' Garima asked Saurav.

'Nothing. Some old friend of his has joined as an intern. I just asked him to introduce me. He got all worked up . . . You have to see her! She is so cute . . . and hot at the same time! She is wearing pink stilettoes to office. Can you beat that?' He said excitedly. 'By the way, where is Shruti?'

'She is at her desk. We are bad company, you see. She will join us for lunch though.'

'Okay . . . but you got to see that girl . . .'

'What was her name?'

'I didn't tell you her name? She is Riya.' He saw her expression change. 'What? You know her?'

'Hmmm . . . I have heard about her from Abhi.'

'What?'

'Don't tell Abhi that I told you, but they were good friends, Abhi had a crush on her and then a big fight took place . . . They don't talk now.'

'Why didn't he tell me about it?'

'He doesn't like to talk about it.'

'Okay . . .'

'Saurav . . . Just be a little careful with her.'

'What?'

'I mean . . . C'mon, we know what you want from girls, right? So, don't end up doing something that you regret later. I am just saying that they were good friends once . . . I hope you are getting it . . .'

'I am not that shallow, Garima. Thanks anyway . . . I will take care.'

He walked off, taken aback and slightly miffed.

'What the fuck?' Shruti said to herself. There was a surplus in the Energy department. The mail said she would be shifted to Infrastructure from the coming week. The worst part.

She would have to report to Dinesh.

She re-read the mail for the fifth time. There was no mistake. It was clearly addressed to her. She looked for Abhi's name in the mail. It was not there. Only she was being shifted. That was the second thing Thapar and Sumita might have discussed the night after she called us to their office.

'This is so unfair.'

'I know,' Abhi said. He felt both relieved and sorry for her. Shruti had gone back to her normal self after a few days. She was sad but she didn't show it as often. She was still working hard as ever.

Sumita's words rung in their head.

You can still make amends. The list still needs to be signed by Thapar. Talk to me sometime. We will see what we can do. Thapar and I.

Ideally, they should have been discussing what Saurav and Garima saw in the parking lot that day, but nobody went near it. Nobody knew what Sumita had in mind. Or Thapar. They feared the worst.

Shruti said everything would be fine. She felt all her hopes dying inside her. It was as if Thapar and Dinesh had already asked her for the favour they'd feared they would. It was as if she had already agreed to it and steeled herself up for it. Refusing them was not an option for her.

'Don't worry, Shruti. Whatever happens, just remember, we are all there for you . . . I hope you know what I mean . . . I will talk to my dad and we will get you out of here . . . you don't . . .' Saurav said.

'Shruti . . . nothing will happen . . . just relax,' Garima added.

'Sir,' she said. Everyone looked around to see Dinesh standing over them.

It had been a week.

'Shruti, Can I see you at my seat?' he said and walked away. Shruti followed him timidly.

Dinesh couldn't help but look down her shirt when Shruti bent down and pulled a chair up to sit next to him. The impression of her black brassiere from over the tight white shirt and her skin hugging trousers sent tingles down his spine.

'So, I hope you have no problems in joining our department.'

'No sir, not at all.'

'There are these six deals that you need to spread,' he said, his voice a lot softer. 'I guess you will be able to do that by tonight.'

'Yes, sir.'

'If there is any problem, you can talk to your friends. Okay?'

'Okay, sir.' She got up and started looking around for her seat. Dinesh saw that and motioned her to her seat. Bang opposite him, only a glass wall separating the two.

Disgust poured from every pore of hers as she adjusted her computer so as to hide from the direct gaze of her new boss.

She worked with her head inside the computer for the rest of the day to avoid any type of eye contact with Dinesh.

She worked hard and fast, just to keep those thoughts out of her mind. Unlike Saurav and Garima, who were still halfway through their day's work, Shruti mailed the work that was assigned to her by eight.

'Done for the day?' Dinesh asked her.

'Yes sir.'

'Going back home?'

'Yes sir.'

'I can drop you if you . . . '

'Sir, I will take the cab . . . '

'*Arey,* not a big deal. Just let me finish off this and we will go. Okay?'

'Sir. but . . . '

'Why? Is there anything bothering you?' Dinesh asked scornfully.

'No sir, actually I was thinking I will go back home with them,' she said and pointed to Saurav and Garima.

'But they are long way from over, I suppose.'

'Sir, I don't mind,' she said coldly.

'Okay, then. Now that you are in office, I will assign you some work. Go to your seat, I will mail you your work,' he said. All the affection in his voice had dried out. 'It is your choice, Shruti. Anyway, it seems like you are quite a workaholic. I like it. Go to your seat now that you don't want a lift home.'

She resisted an urge to hit him across his face. She felt disgusted. She felt as if she was already touched by him.

Shruti checked her mail. The work would take three days. She had a hunch that life would change now. For worse. She often thought what wrong had she done, which made her deserve this.

A few tears left her eyes.

Saurav and Garima came to her seat as soon as Dinesh left. They'd heard the conversation. Abhi joined them too.

They all looked at her, as she looked at them teary eyed, and though no words were exchanged, they let her know that they were with her no matter what. That moment defined what they meant for each other, their relationship. They were a family.

They went back to their seats, thanked their stars for the friends they had, recounted the times they had spent together and day dreamed about the times to come.

Days were getting tougher for Shruti after the snub she gave Dinesh.

She worked nights through her toe curling painful periods. She missed Garima's birthday, so none of them celebrated it.

Her average hours clocked 89 hours for the next week. She went home just twice that week.

What was even worse was that she knew all this would count for naught if she did not give in to what Dinesh and Thapar really wanted from her.

What was even more painful was that Dinesh used to leave office very early, and would not forget to ask how her work was progressing.

Dinesh's attitude towards her was getting maniacal by the day as he kept crushing her under piles of work.

Meanwhile, the subprime losses were starting to hit all major banks and economies.

The whole hoopla about subprime losses is simple. You lend money to gun totting, tattoo pierced man to buy a big house hoping that he would pay you back well in time.

Obviously the man ended up in jail after few months. So there was no way the banks could get the money back.

Take millions of these cases and scores of banks and you will get the picture.

The banks weren't getting their money back.

The banks lose money; the investors in those banks lose money. The lesser money in the market, that is in your pocket, the lesser you spend. The car you meant to buy a few months back would still be standing the showroom now. So what does the car manufacturers do? Stop producing. What do the workers of the company do?

They get laid off!

So, at the end of the day, everybody goes broke and becomes jobless!

# What Is Going On Here?

'Oh yes, Riya. Abhi talks a lot about you,' Saurav said. He was toying with the idea of approaching her for the last few days but he held back thinking that Abhi might agree to introduce him to Riya. A week passed before he finally made the move.

'Does he?' Riya asked.

'Oh yes, he surely does.'

'That is nice to hear, sir.'

'So, is there a training that you guys are going under?' he asked.

'No. they have put us under some people and we do some of their work. Basically, getting acquainted with how things work.'

'Nice.'

'Sir, how is the work here? I mean the culture and all . . . I have heard they have their own stylist here . . . I asked someone and she didn't know! She of course didn't, looking at her extra-large handbag and green mascara with red nail paint . . . who does that these days . . .?'

Saurav kept looking at her glossy lips form those words, not listening to a word that she had to say.

'Sir? Sir?' She waved her hand in his face and broke his stare.

'Huh?'

'Sir?'

'Oh . . . stylist . . . yes . . . fourth floor . . . to the right . . . you don't need her . . . You look fine.'

'Thank you . . . that is so sweet of you. No, I just want to meet her once and ask her if she is blind . . . I mean there are so many girls who wear ballerina shoes with . . .'

She went on again. Saurav lost his mind again.

'Saurav? Sir . . . I really need to go . . . My boss . . . she is a real bitch . . . Kritika . . . know her? It is better that you stay away from her . . . Okay . . . bye.'

'Huh? Yeah . . . bye.' They shook hands and she walked away from him. Saurav had never seen anybody walk so perfectly well on five inch pumps. Pink pumps. They were a different shade from what he had seen her wearing the day before.

Abhi was neck deep in work that day. Sameer was disappointed with his team's performance and had decided to make amends. He had buried everybody under him with loads of work. Though he had not yet stooped to Dinesh's levels. He was profusely apologetic about the workload and was always the last one to leave office.

Abhi was scrolling through his mailbox when Saurav tapped on his shoulder.

'Look whom have I got?' he said and pointed towards Riya, who was standing right beside him.

'Hi!' she said.

'Ummm . . . Hi . . . ' he said.

'How are you? It's been so long . . . and you have grown so . . .' Riya asked.

'I am fine.'

'Thank me, I made the two of you meet. I will get a chair for myself. Will you have anything?' Saurav asked.

'Hmm . . . Saurav . . . I need to go . . . I have work . . .' Abhi said.

'*Arey,* sit for a while . . .'

'Saurav I need to go . . . now . . .' Abhi said and got up.

'You can . . .'

'I can't . . .' he said and left, without looking at Riya even once. He left them in an awkward silence.

'He does *not* talk about me, does he?' Riya asked, with little beads in her eyes.

Saurav hung his head and said, 'No, he does not.'

A couple of weeks passed and Garima felt bad about it, when she heard what had happened.

'Why did you walk away?' Garima asked Abhi. He was staying over at her place that night.

'Did Saurav talk to you about it?'

'Yes, he did.'

'He talks to you?'

For the last two weeks—precisely from the time Riya stepped into the office—Saurav had been ignoring the other three. He was keeping out of sight of Abhi and was often spotted at the cafeteria with Riya.

'Don't say that.'

'Why shouldn't I? It's been more than a week and I don't think he has been with us.'

'Abhi? What is the problem?'

'I don't want to talk about it. By the way, where is Shruti, man? She leaves home early and doesn't pick her phone. Dinesh let the steam off her?'

'Yes, he has. Sort of. And don't change the topic.'

'I am not. I told you I am not talking about it.'

'You are irritating me.'

'Why the hell are you getting irritated?'

'You feel bad about your friend talking to a friend who talks to an ex-crush of yours. What am I to make of it? Are you jealous? All I am asking is whether you still have a problem of some other guy talking to her?'

'Saurav is not some other guy.' He got up and looked the other way.

'But you have a problem, right?'

'Yes.'

'Fine.' She threw the cushion she was holding on the ground and went to her room slamming the door behind her.

Abhi kept standing there.

It was late at night when Abhi went to her room and sat where she was sleeping. Her pillow was a little wet with her tears.

He bent over and whispered in her ears, 'Love you. I am sorry.'

'Love you too.' She opened her eyes. She had been waiting for him to come to her for the last hour. 'But couldn't you have come and said that earlier?'

'Yes . . . and I don't care about her. Just that, I don't want her around . . .' he paused. 'They can't be together . . . I mean

. . . you know what Saurav wants . . . and she is silly . . . she doesn't know . . .'

'Come here.' She pulled him close and planted a kiss on his lips.

They hugged each other and went off to sleep. Or did not.

I had been looking for a job for the last two weeks but I was not getting anywhere with it.

After days of nothingness, I finally landed myself an interview with an analytics firm where Sameer's wife had worked in. I dressed in a sharp fitted suit for the interview. The slight beard was gotten rid of. Avantika gave me all kinds of threats before I did it.

'Why not call everyone home for a party someday?' I said as I admired myself in the mirror. I wasn't the most super looking guy, but when you have a girl like Avantika by your side, you tend to think otherwise.

'I don't see them spending much time together.'

'Why?'

'I mean Saurav and Abhi have something going on between them. I was thinking of talking to Garima about it, but it always slips my mind.' She came near and smelled me. 'Nice. You will do well.' She pecked me.

'And Shruti . . . Dinesh still on her case?'

'I am a little worried about her.'

'Why?'

'Dinesh is a bastard and he has let her off the hook . . . all of a sudden . . . It's weird . . .'

'Guilt pangs?'

'You know that he is not that kind of a guy.'

'Very strange,' I said as I grabbed Avantika

'Hmm . . . very,' she said as we kissed. 'Not now . . .'

'Why not?'

'You get through.'

'That is what I am meaning to do,' I said as I pushed her to the wall.

'Get through the interview. Tonight.'

'What tonight?'

'Whatever you want.'

'Promise?'

'Promise.'

I left for the interview.

Sameer's wife was very popular in the firm, it seemed. The interview looked and felt like a mere formality. I was in. I was promptly given the offer letter, and it seemed like they had it ready before the interview.

I wasn't the smartest or the brainiest guy around. But I knew the right people! And was probably lucky.

The drop was huge. From 2.4 million to 0.6 million, but the perks were huge.

Good people.

Sleep.

Sanity.

Weeks passed by and Saurav was falling in love with Riya. He knew he was ignoring the other three but he thought he would make up for the lost time when Riya goes back to Delhi.

Sometimes, it was a new key ring with a cute teddy hanging from it while on the others it was a coffee mug with Riya written on it. Every day there was some surprise or the other waiting for Riya on her table. Soon, her table drawers were full of baubles, trinkets, cards and the like. Riya had started liking Saurav too but she was more than a little wary of falling for him.

It was their umpteenth dinner date together.

'I really like you. I mean, I have made it a little too obvious, haven't I?'

'Hmm . . . not really . . . fifty three gifts count? I would have to say, NO!' she giggled.

'Okay . . . I get it. But you are still to say what you feel about all this? I mean me, us, the whole thing that is going around.'

'You know, I find you very nice, Saurav. It is just that I don't feel it is right. You know what happened with Abhi. And we are still not over it. I mean he is still very angry with me. It seems . . .'

'But that was a long time ago, man! He is happy now . . . he has Garima now, doesn't he? And do you think it is fair? I mean, why should I be the one to carry the burden of his or your past? And, I am sure you will sort it out someday.'

'I hope so.'

'You will.'

'Okay, I think it is getting late. I must go,' Riya said.

'You are not going today.'

'What?'

'You are coming to my place today.'

'Oh . . . I am not.'

'Yes, you are . . .'

'But I can't. Please don't force me . . . Some other time . . . we can go out to this really nice place in Banjara . . . it has really nice pasta . . . and we can go shopping tomorrow . . . there is this new place . . . and I . . .'

'I am not forcing you. I am requesting. Next, I will be begging you.'

'Please don't. I have to go.'

'Now that you are acting extremely stubborn, I will have to tell you, I have planned a big surprise at my place.'

'*What?*'

'Yes, a big surprise.'

'That is not going to work, Saurav. I am going home.'

'I swear.'

'Seriously?'

'Yes.'

'And I have to come?'

'Yes, obviously. It is for you.'

'It had better be a good one,' she said and smiled at him.

They reached his place and he was unlocking the door when he said, 'See, I planned it well, if something goes wrong, it would not be because of me, but people who helped me out in this.'

They moved into the house. Nothing had gone wrong; it was looking exactly the way he wanted it to.

His huge drawing room was lit in bright yellow. The candles glowed bright, placed all across the perimeter of the room, the window sills, and every possible place. Different sizes, different levels. Big thick red candles were on the TV stand where there was no TV now. A table was placed bang in the centre of the room. There was a huge cake on the table waiting alongside a glass trough filled with water, which had green and red floating candles in it.

'Nice. It is so nice. But . . .' she said, covering her mouth in disbelief.

'Yes . . . go on . . .'

'I really like it! It is so . . . nice and . . . lovely . . .'

'Thank you.'

'But *why*?'

'Because . . .' he turned her around and faced her. 'I really love you . . . and someday, I would like to have your life as lit up as this room is right now. I hope to make each day of your life as special as this day is. I hope to make you the happiest you can be, happier than you have ever been. But before I do it, I want to give you something that will remind you of this day,' he said and started to dig in his pocket for something. And out came a ring box.

'DO NOT tell me,' she said and looked heaven wards.

'Miss Riya Sharma, will you some day—if I prove to be good boyfriend and all that stuff—and we complete very many years of courtship, marry me?' he asked, half bent.

'Are you crazy? Look at that ring Saurav. I can't take that. It looks so damn expensive. What will I tell my mom . . .? Which one is it . . .? Oh . . . I have seen it . . . but this is so . . .'

'Are you . . .? Is that a yes or a no?'

'I can't take that ring, Saurav. Seriously.'

'Answer THE QUESTION! The ring is not important.'

'Oh . . . yeah, yeah . . . obviously . . .' she said, too distracted by the look of the ring. It was a gold ring with a flower shaped diamond and Ruby of the same shape. 'I mean, yes. I mean, I love you too. I do. I mean, I think I do.'

'That will do,' Saurav said ad got up. 'And you have to accept this.'

'I can't.'

'Let us drop this utterly futile discussion about a stupid ring.'

'It is not stupid. It is beautiful!'

'And me?'

'You are so cute.' They hugged.

'The cake,' Saurav muttered.

'The stupid cake,' she said and hugged him tighter.

'It is a chocolate cake.'

'You are my chocolate cake,' she said and kissed him on his cheek.

They always say it is better to be with someone who loves you than to be with someone whom you love.

It helps when your boyfriend whips out a diamond ring to propose to you. Has to work.

We entered the plush Taj Banjara hotel. It had been quite a while since the two of us had gone out for a dinner date. By ourselves.

We picked a window seat in the café and huddled our asses in the cushioned seats. I wanted her ass on *me*, though.

'You know what?'

'What?' I asked.

'I am jealous.'

'Of?'

'You.'

'Why so?'

'Your new job. I wish I could join your firm too . . .'

'I know. But the money . . .'

'When did you start caring about the money?'

'I don't, but you are so well paid there . . . and the dip is not worth it. You have worked hard for this, Avantika.'

'That is why. I don't want to work hard anymore.'

'Very early retirement?'

'I wish.'

'And what do plan to do post retirement?'

'Stay at home.'

'Stay at home and do what?'

'I will let you know that tonight Mr Deb.' She looked in to my eyes as if she would eat me up. I wouldn't have any problem with that.

'Let me know right now about your devious plans. I am so anxious.'

'You wouldn't want a tent in you shorts,' she said and moved her fingers up my thigh.

'I would love that.' I wanted to go home right then.

'I would not. Let's order. Keep something for the night,' she said.

'Yes . . . sure.'

We went through the whole menu to choose what we always ordered, Chicken lasagne, Mint and chocolate Oreo shakes and a Penne Arabiatta.

We sat and waited until the order came. The topic of discussion was whether Avantika's parents would have any problem with the fact that I earned less than her. It was declared to be a non-issue and nobody needed to know how much I earned.

'Shit . . . I knew this . . .' Avantika said as she dropped her fork on to her plate, and looked far in to the distance.

'What?' I looked up.

'Look there.'

'Where?'

'There . . .'

'Oh . . . *what*? What the fuck? Is she . . .? Oh shit!'

In the distance, we saw what we all had feared. We saw Dinesh walking with a beautiful girl in a short skirt enter the hip club of Taj Banjara.

The girl was Shruti.

# They Are So Cooked

*Lehman brothers goes bankrupt.*

*AIG in deep trouble.*

*Barclays in deeper trouble.*

The news screamed out loud.

All investment banks had taken a hit. Twenty two thousand employees of Lehman were thrown out in a space of a week. All of them were dollar millionaires.

AIG had cut ten thousand jobs. Citigroup had laid down twenty thousand workers.

Silverman Finance was next.

Riya had started falling hard and fast for Saurav. Saurav had really turned on the charm after the surprise he had given her at his place and she was no longer wary of acting as his girlfriend. She had avoided talking to him in office for the simple reason that Abhi might spot them, but now she hardly thought twice before hugging him.

Abhi had noticed them more than once. And every time, it

resulted in the same strange churning of stomach. It had been almost a month that he and Saurav had talked and it didn't seem like they would anytime soon.

Abhi and Garima chose a different seat from where Saurav and Riya were sitting. Shruti was nowhere to be seen. She was probably working. They had started noticing that she and Dinesh left within a few minutes of one another every day.

Abhi had followed her once but he saw her getting into the cab she always went home in. Maybe they meet at somewhere else, they thought.

Both of them were disgusted with her behaviour. They often thought of asking her, but something stopped them from doing so.

Everyone was eating peacefully at the cafeteria when the volume of the TV set was turned out loud.

Everybody looked up to see what was happening.

They knew now why the volume was turned up. A nice looking female on Headlines Today was reading out the Breaking News from a Teleprompter.

"*Close on the heels of banking giant Citibank's decision to eliminate around 20,000 jobs worldwide, the Silverman Finance is reported to be planning to cut around 10,000 jobs from its investment banking business in the coming weeks.*

*Silverman Finance is planning a reduction of 10,000 staff in the coming weeks, mostly from its global banking and markets workforce that spans around 50 countries, including India.*

*It said that jobs were likely to be cut in the city of Hyderabad, adding that Silverman Finance's high street operations and that of its subsidiary Natwon would remain unaffected. Silverman Finance employs around 1.7 lakh people, of which around a 4,000 are in India.*

*The newspaper also reported that Silverman Finance would cut around 15 per cent of its global banking and markets work force, while saying that the move would not affect employees from the US, and would mainly centre on Silverman Finance's investment banking arm.*

*The report of planned job cuts . . .* "

There was pin drop silence in the room for the next few minutes. The room turned cold and the conversations stopped. An uneasy silence gripped the room. Every look turned in to a stare. The feeling of who will be sacked and who will stay, gripped everyone.

Everybody in Silverman Finance may have done a million things, but out of those, one thing was common—they had cribbed about their job.

But now, everyone realized how much they loved their job. One in every two employees would go. Lose his or her job. Lose the life he or she was accustomed to.

Thapar was right. I was lucky. I had more time than others to look for a job. And lesser competition.

Within the next few minutes, a meeting of IBD was called.

Thereafter, Thapar gave an awful speech about how things would be fine and left no impact whatsoever on anyone who was listening in. The tension and anticipation was palpable.

The respect now shown to Sumita was seen to be believed. Everyone who saw her didn't forget to tell her how young she looked or how pleased they were to talk to her.

# Of Broken Hearts and Smashed Heads

'I don't know . . .' Abhi said. 'If they throw us out, which they probably will, I have no idea what I will do . . .'

Garima had called up Saurav and Shruti and had forced them to take time for this night at Abhi's place.

They were all there, but there were hardly any words exchanged before Abhi had asked this question.

'Nothing will happen. It will do us no good to think about it . . .' Garima said.

'Saurav will go to Delhi, of course.' Abhi said sarcastically. 'So will you . . .' he looked at Garima and said.

'Whatever,' Saurav said as he sipped his beer.

'I can't go back . . .' Shruti.

Abhi and Garima exchanged a wry expression for they knew that she had kept her manager in her pocket, for however she might have done it. She wouldn't lose her job for sure.

'You don't need to. Dinesh would do anything to keep you in,' Abhi said.

'What?'

'Nothing.'

'Why are you saying that?'

'You know why. I am not talking about this.'

'No, tell me.'

'You know it Shruti. Deb sir saw you with Dinesh at the Taj.'

'What? ' Saurav butted in, shocked.

'Yes, so?'

'Is it true?' Saurav asked.

'Yes,' Abhi said. 'And leaving with him every day? Every single day you left within minutes of him leaving the office.'

'So, what? Don't you go out with Garima? And Saurav and that new intern, Riya? If you can go out, then why not me? It has been a month since we hung out together. Every one of you was busy. Why should I be alone? Why should I be the one sitting at home and waiting for the three of you to at least pick up my calls? But no, you are either with Garima, Saurav with Riya or your phones are busy. You guys don't even call back.'

'We had been busy . . .'

'Garima, busy enough that Abhi stayed over at your place night after night. And Saurav, when was the last time you came to my seat? I don't even want to talk about it. I just don't. Anyway, Dinesh is not as bad as we thought him to be. He helped me. And he helped you too.'

'Helped us? What the fuck do you mean?'

'Don't swear, Saurav. I requested him to keep the load down on us. Can't you see it? I asked him as a friend and he did it.'

'I don't want the load to be down if it had be like this way. And you call him a *friend*?'

'Saurav, I think you are blowing it out of proportion.'

'Whatever you might say, Shruti. We are concerned about you. We don't want you to . . . ' Abhi said

'What is wrong with you?' Shruti asked, irritated.

'What is wrong with *us*? You are bloody sleeping with your bastard boss, that's what's wrong,' Saurav said.

'For heaven, sake . . . ' Shruti threw her hands in the air and got up. 'You really think so? We are just friends. *Just friends.*'

'Friends? Friends who sleep together? You hated him and now you call him your friend? What do you do with him? Play chess? I don't think so! We all know what happens in the car park. We have seen it. We all have. I told you I would get you a job. I fucking told you. You didn't have to go to him.'

'Could you have asked me at least?' Shruti said. 'How the hell did you even think . . . He is just a . . .'

'What is there to ask? You fucking went out with him! I don't care whether you slept with him or not. But you fucking hated him! So now . . . *why*? And you call *him* a *friend*. What are *we*?' Abhi shouted.

'I think you really deserve what you are getting, Shruti. The bastard in Delhi you are going to marry. I pity that guy. He should have known better. What the fuck Shruti? You have let me down . . . you have let us down . . . You are so . . . I don't want to see your face ever again. Leave this room right now. You have fucking insulted me. Us all. You know what he put us through. And what? You called him a friend? A friend, Shruti? Why the hell did you have to go and sleep with him? I would have given you all the money. I would have man . . . just go to hell. It is all about the money, isn't it? Everything for you . . . you should have asked me . . . just once . . . *Dinesh?* Everything is about you . . . isn't it? Just like your parents said . . .' Saurav said.

'I had no other choice,' she said and left the house, banging the door behind her.

'You always have a choice,' Abhi said as she left.

Silence gripped the room. Everybody looked at each other as if to ask the question of whether they had gone a little too far.

Abhi thought he had not. The very fact that she met their most hated guy outside office angered him beyond limit. Garima was still angry but not so much.

Saurav was too dazed to think anything. Only if they had thought about things from her perspective. They had left her alone.

'Did we say too much?' Garima asked.

'No,' Saurav said.

'I think so. Saurav said too much,' Abhi said.

'I said too much? Are you crazy? And why the hell didn't you guys tell me about this before?' Saurav asked.

'If only you got time out for us, from that girlfriend of yours.'

'Her name is Riya.'

'Whatever her name is. I don't care,' Abhi said and got up. 'The bottom line is that you are the one who fucking said too much. That too when you hardly knew anything. You think you are very smart because you could land a girl I couldn't . . . with all that money and stupid gifts of yours.'

'Don't act childish.'

'I am not.'

'Oh . . . yes you are.'

'Will you fight with me for that girl of yours? That fucking girl of yours?'

'She is Riya.'

'I know what she is. I know her. And I know what kind of girl she is.'

'What the fuck do you mean?'

'What? You wanted a girl to have fun with . . . she is yours! She has done that before . . . so go ahead . . . do it.'

'I know everything about her.'

'You know shit about her,' Abhi said as his temper peaked. 'Ask her what all she did with Arjun,'

'Shut up, Abhi, you are sick.'

'What sick? Ask her.'

'For god's sake! He was her boyfriend.'

'So what is the fucking difference? Why the double standards? Shruti slept with Dinesh to keep her job safe that is so not acceptable to you. But when your girl sleeps with her awesomely rich boyfriend just to keep him from going away, that is acceptable?'

'*What the hell?* She did *not* sleep with him. And even if she did, I don't give a damn.'

'Guys!' Garima shouted to keep them from shouting.

'No, let him speak, Garima. I didn't know Abhi could say such things about his friends . . . Maybe tomorrow he will say the same about you . . .'

'Friends, my foot! She is not my friend. Never was. She doesn't even know what friendship is. That bitch . . . And dare you fucking say anything about Garima . . .'

'You are such a bastard, Abhi . . .'

'Fuck off, man! You will come to know when she leaves you someday . . . and we won't be here . . .'

'She won't,' Saurav said and turned around to leave.

'I wish she does. And where you are going? Oh, to her? Don't forget to fuck her. She will be ready to do it. Just tell her you will dump her otherwise.'

Saurav turned back and rushed towards Abhi and rammed

his head on to Abhi chest. Abhi staggered and moved backwards towards the wall, stepped on a glass which broke beneath his feet and banged his head on the wall. He fell on the ground and immediately a pool of blood formed where his head lay.

'That is what you deserve, bastard,' Saurav said as he looked down at him. The very next second he realized that Abhi was hurt. As he bent to see the damage, he was slapped hard by Garima, who was now in tears.

'Get the hell away from him!'

'But . . .'

'Just go away,' she wailed out loud and bent down on Abhi who had almost blanked out.

'Ga—'

'Get out! Get *out*!' She stood up and grabbed Saurav by his hand. 'Get the hell out of my house and don't come back here again.' She pushed him outside the door and shouted, 'Don't ever come near him or me. Ever again.' She banged the door on his face and went back to see Abhi. He was helping himself up against the wall, his head smashed and glass pieces lodged inside his bottom of the feet.

Garima kept herself from fainting seeing all the blood around and her stomach churned to see the glass pieces sticking out of Abhi's feet.

It took half an hour for the paramedics to arrive. Till then, Garima cradled Abhi's head—which was no longer bleeding but there was deep wound instead—and kept crying.

The glass or the wound didn't hurt as much.

The glass was shattered. So was their family.

Abhi spent the next day in hospital. There were thirteen stitches on his feet and four on his head. A bandage was wrapped around his head like a bandana and he was asked not to keep his foot down for the next week or so. Neither Saurav nor Shruti asked how Abhi was. Dinesh asked, though. Sameer, Avantika and I had gone to visit him to see how he was.

Garima also took off for the next two days, but came to the office on the third. Whenever Garima saw Dinesh now, she had an inherent feeling to snuff the life out of him.

Finally, on the fourth day, Abhi came to office. He was limping on one foot, and had a hockey stick in hand. Sameer had asked him to stay at home but he would not listen. It was partly because his job was on the line and mostly because once Garima had called from office and cried because she had no one else to talk to. She had filled up Abhi's inbox with mails about how much she missed him. Abhi told her that if they were to lose this job they would do it together.

The four of them did not meet that day.

They took different seats in the cafeteria.

Abhi and Garima sat in one corner. Saurav sat in one with Riya, who was crying softly. Shruti was in another with the team.

Sometimes, they exchanged glances but when they saw the other person looking their way, they turned away.

Everybody had found people to bitch about the others.

'I don't want to talk about them. Can we talk about something else?' Shruti asked. This was her fourth conversation with the Silverman guy who lived next door. Not to mention he had the hots for her.

'No please. You've got to tell me.'

'Why do you want to know?'

'I don't want to. I need to know.' He tried the sympathy card.

'Why?'

'Because I need to know what is bothering you so much.'

'Nothing. It is just that they thought I was sleeping with my boss. All I wanted to do was help myself. And they didn't even bother to ask! '

'Maybe you should have talked to them.'

'What talk to them? I don't need to tell them everything. And I don't need to tell you everything.'

'Why don't you talk to them now?'

'That chapter is over. Forever. I don't want to talk to them ever. Let's talk about something else.'

'Okay.'

She dozed off twenty minutes later. Rahul could do nothing but depress her further.

She saw him leave the room. She got up and wrecked the room, throwing everything around and shouting out loud before she sank on the floor and cried the night away. She stared at the kitchen and the knife that was there . . .

It wasn't over yet. She cried a little more.

Abhi and Garima had tried to avoid talking about Saurav or Shruti following that day.

'You have nothing to say?' Garima asked.

'About?'

'That day.'

'No.'

'Hmm . . . ' Silence gripped them for the next few minutes.

'It is Saurav's birthday today.'

'I know,' Garima said. 'I don't think we are wishing him. I am not. After what he did to you, he didn't even have the decency to at least come and see you once.'

'Hmm . . .'

'No, I am serious, Abhi. He saw what happened. You were bleeding from everywhere . . . It is not like he doesn't know. And that friend of yours . . . she didn't even think once . . .'

'Hmm . . . . even Shruti didn't. But I think we said a little too much. But she didn't do the right thing . . . I mean, it is unimaginable . . .'

'I do not know. That was the last day I talked to them. I so hate them. It's not as if they don't matter to me. They do. And that is why I hate them more,' Garima said as she adjusted Abhi's bandage.

'Hmm . . . But where is Shruti? I haven't seen her in office.'

'Maybe Dinesh knows. Who cares?'

Saurav spent the night consoling Riya that it was not her fault and that Abhi was a selfish, jealous bastard. Not that it made any difference to her or her crying, but it made Saurav hate Abhi even more with every passing second. He didn't like the fact that Riya was crying because of him. Moreover, he knew that he would have to choose between her and Abhi. And a million times over, he would choose Riya.

The buzz about layoffs was gaining ground as days passed by. It was now official; half the teams would go. People who had eternally hated their jobs with all their heart were now mortally scared.

Some of the new joinees had started looking for new houses. Small affordable ones. Many had updated their CVs and had started forwarding it to their friends in lesser organizations who were having a field day to see these overpaid pigs suffer.

Tragedy brings people closer and this was happening in Silverman Finance long before it actually struck. People who sat in adjacent cabins but never talked were now talking about everything from which schools their children went to and whether they had applied to any place else just in case they lost this job.

Nobody had anything else to do in those fifteen days.

Abhi had panicked big time after reading the official announcement of the layoffs, but Garima said he could join her father's business if he wanted to. Garima had already told her parents about Abhi and they were only too happy to hear their daughter sound happy again.

And to think of it, losing the job was no longer that bad an option for him. He had his life set, a business of his own. Having a rich girlfriend helps. Abhi now had one, just like he mentioned to Saurav, that he had wanted one.

# Things Turn Bad

It was the first time that she was doing this.

And it wasn't Delhi or Chandigarh. The people jostling for bottles were rickshaw pullers and labourers, half of whom had forgotten what they had ordered when they saw her approaching.

She pulled down her T-shirt and tried to be extremely loud and confident.

'Smirnoff vodka. Full.' She took out her cell phone and yakked loudly. '*Haan*, bring the car around. Ask Amit and Rajat to come. Make it quick, man.' She then went ahead and ordered two beers. It lent more weight to story that there were three guys coming to join her.

She put them all in her huge red and golden handbag and quickly turned around the corner. She took an auto rickshaw and headed home.

A senior had come up to her earlier that day and asked whether it was fun doing it with Dinesh. While he walked away, telling her that it was her friend who told him everything about her and Dinesh. She kept sitting there open mouthed, waiting for it to register. She turned towards the computer as tears trickled down her cheek. She could see it in the reflection of her computer screen. A group formed around that guy who had just talked to her and then everyone looked at her and then either smiled, smirked or expressed shock. She felt all those eyes on her. As if they were stripping her, there and then.

She had never expected they could leak out such a thing. She clenched her fist till her nails clawed inside her palms.

She prayed for the driver to drive fast. The crowns were peeking from the top of it as she clutched on to it tightly. The speed breaker clanged the bottles together and made the driver look at her in the rear mirror. It was a sweating Shruti.

As soon as she reached the apartment gate, she gave the driver a hundred rupee note and rushed to her apartment.

She missed Saurav. Abhi. Garima. Me, probably!

She wanted to fight it. She wanted to tell herself she could do without them.

That's when she decided to drink that night. Alone.

She took out the bottles and kept them on the table.

She never drank beer. It is a guys' drink, Saurav once told her.

Chauvinistic pig, she thought.

And wondered why she had not seen that before. He was nothing but a female bashing asshole.

Shruti opened the bottle and the stench made her crook her nose. She held the bottle in both her hands and took a long gulp.

She coughed and cringed while the yellow liquid made its way down her throat, spoiling the taste of her tongue for the rest of the night.

She got hold of the bottle again and gulped in down in three huge sips.

She felt nauseous. And tipsy.

Shruti ran over her phone. She looked for Abhi's number. It wasn't in the last dialled numbers. Or received. Nor missed calls. Neither was Saurav's or Garima's.

She found Garima's number and pressed the dial button.

And cut the phone.

She did it thrice and then threw way her phone which hit the skirting of the room. The battery and the keypad spilled out.

She had expected Garima to call. She had expected Avantika to call.

Nobody did.

She wouldn't call either.

The two remaining bottles were opened and a glass was filled—half with vodka and the rest with beer.

She drank it down.

It tasted terrible and it felt terrible. Her throat burned. Her stomach churned.

But she felt light.

She was doing fine. She could do without them. She could sleep with Dinesh. Why should they care?

She made herself another one. It burned her insides. She felt hot in her stomach. She felt good in her mind. She was free.

She kept smiling incessantly. Thinking of all the times they had spent together. And thinking about how much she hated them now.

With the third drink in, she puked.

The next day, she resigned.

# Things Get Ugly

It had been three days and three nights that Shruti had been drinking.

It was the same time after which Abhi and Garima had noticed that her table was empty. Everything from the mug which had the photograph of the four of them together to the photo of Shruti with her brother was gone.

They looked across the computer and Dinesh knew what they would ask.

'She resigned.'

'When?'

'Three days back.'

'Why?' they both asked.

'You should know. She wasn't looking very good and was mumbling something . . . about you guys . . . Don't know. But you should ask her.'

Garima covered her mouth and barely kept from crying. Tears ran down her cheeks.

'We were wrong,' she said, not looking at Abhi.

'But why did she resign?'

'Can't you see it?'

'She wanted to show us that we were wrong.'

'I don't think so.'

'Abhi, are you fucking wrong in the head?' she shouted and saw everyone look at them. She mellowed down and continued, 'We were wrong. Then and even now. Can't you see it? Put your ego aside and see. Had she been sucking up to Dinesh, she would have done it even now. Why should she leave the job? You know this for a fact that she would die but not give up this job.'

'Maybe . . .'

'Abhi . . . Think. She left because of us! I had you. You had me. Saurav had Riya. She was the one alone. She was the one who wanted us the most. And we know that she needed the job more than everyone of us. She was the only one who wasn't tired of getting fucked here day and night. She couldn't have resigned for any other reason.'

'But she doesn't look the type . . .'

'How can you . . .? Leave it. You don't look the type who would fight with your best friend over a girl . . .'

'What the fuck? He was the one who . . .'

'Leave that . . . I am sorry.'

'So? What do we do now?' Abhi asked.

'I don't know, Abhi. You and Saurav need to talk to her. Salvage whatever is left . . . if there is anything left . . .'

'You go talk to Saurav. I will order a cab.'

'No Abhi. *You* talk to Saurav. I will order a cab.'

'I won't.'

'For heaven's sake, Abhi! Will you stop acting selfish now? Put your stupid ego aside and call Saurav up. Look where it got us.' She got up and left.

Abhi fiddled with the phone for the next ten minutes as he tried to string words to say. He still did not want to call up Saurav when he eventually did, images of what had happened that day came back to him.

After Saurav did not pick up the call twice, Abhi gave a second thought of calling him up again. However, he eventually did and Saurav picked up.

'*Bol*,' Saurav said. He still sounded pissed, though he was relieved to get a call from him in all these days.

'Shruti has resigned.'

'*What?*'

'Yes.'

'So?' Saurav tried to contain in his shock.

'Garima says it's because of us.'

'What the fuck . . .? This is bullshit . . . .'

'I think what she is saying is right . . .'

'Do you?'

'Yes.'

Their tones were becoming normal with every sentence they exchanged.

'We are going to her place. Now. Garima has ordered a cab. See you at the main gate.'

'Okay.'

On the way to the gate, Saurav went to Dinesh's seat. He turned his chair and looked into his eyes and had asked furiously, 'What did you do with her? Tell me or I am going to smash your head into the computer screen. Did you ever . . . ever . . . ever . . . ever . . . touch Shruti?'

'Excuse me?'

'Tell me.' Saurav bellowed.

'Are you nuts or what? She has always been like my sister. She always reminded me of her. I am really sorry for her resignation. She really needed the job. I wanted . . .'

'How the fuck do you know?'

'She told me. She is a sweet kid. I was thinking of making her the sub junior analyst. That is why I piled her with work, but seems like she had more issues at hand.'

'*What?* Then why did you ask her once to leave with you? In your car . . . the one which Thapar uses . . . We know about it sir . . . Why?'

'That? You got me all wrong, Saurav. We all knew Thapar wanted Shruti. I asked him to leave her for me and he did that as a favour to all the times he had used my car for his ghastly acts. I just wanted Thapar to know that I am with her. I didn't want her to go through what the other girls went through. But seems like fate had something else decided for her . . . I am sorry for her . . . I tried . . .'

'We spotted you at Taj . . .'

'She treated me when I broke her the news of recommending her for the post of sub junior . . .'

Hearing this, Saurav rushed downstairs after shouting a loud thank you to him and hugging the life out of him.

He came down the stairs and said, 'We were wrong. Dinesh is the good guy.'

They left for Shruti's place and Saurav explained what he knew to the other two, who were now neck deep in guilt.

Nobody exchanged a word in car.

They trudged their feet through the stairs to her apartment. Everyone was thinking of what they would say to her. Abhi and Saurav wished they were Garima because she was already in tears and they knew that this would be the thing she would do there.

Cry. Cry her heart out.

They were a few feet away and nobody took the lead to go ahead and press the bell.

Garima pushed Abhi to go ahead. He fumbled a few steps and walked up the door.

The door was slightly ajar. Abhi hit the bell and waited. No answer.

He hit the bell a few more times and there was still no answer.

Abhi pushed the door open and a strange putrid stench hit their noses. The kind that makes you launch into physical convulsions.

As soon as it reached Saurav's nose, he barged in, half out of reflex and half out of fear. He looked around in the drawing room. She wasn't there. Her phone lay smashed in a corner.

He ran to her bedroom. She wasn't there and the room was unlocked.

He had heard that bathrooms were the place girls often chose to . . . He banished those thoughts from his mind and went ahead.

Saurav walked up the bathroom door and looked back to see Abhi and Garima staring at him. He was petrified and the fear in Abhi's and Garima's eyes didn't make it any bit easier.

He slightly opened the bathroom door and it creaked. His pulse shot up and he slammed open the door.

Empty.

They all let their breaths out and stood there for a while.

They rummaged through her stuff to find anything substantial.

They went to the drawing room and noticed what they had missed. They had trampled all over the dried remains of Shruti's puke.

Hell lots of it.

There were neatly stacked bottles of vodka and beer in the corner.

Saurav guessed she had been drinking at least for a week.

What they did not know was that it had been just three days.

They sat down on the couch and waited for her to return. Shruti was out to party that day.

During the last three days, there was hardly a moment when she wasn't drunk. And though Rahul had not being able to do anything that he intended to do with her, he was still sticking with her, trying for the last day and a half to slip a hand in, or get close to her in any which way possible.

And got abused in half a dozen languages with different degrees of slurri*ness* in speech.

That day, they were in *Elan*, the grandest disco in whole of Hyderabad. Two of its floors were complete and after the third, it would be the biggest club in Asia.

Blue lights, short skirts and a huge bar—Rahul fancied his chances here. There was so much snogging around that Rahul thought this was the place where he could seduce her into something silly.

They sat down on a corner table and she slumped on the table immediately.

'Are you okay?'

'I need something to drink.'

'What will you have?

'Vodka. With nothing,' she looked at him and laughed aloud. 'Vodka, asshole, *jaldi.*'

'Shruti, don't swear.'

'Don't you think that is cool? Saurav thought it was cool for girls to swear,' she said as she put her chin on her outstretched hand on the table.

'I will get your drink.'

She went off to sleep by the time he got her the drink. He kept the drink on the table and came and sat very close to her. He put a hand across her shoulder and leaned on to her. She pushed him away as he leant further in.

This happened a few more times. And finally . . . Rahul, overcome by lust and stupidity, let his hand slip down from her neck and got that inside her T shirt.

It woke her up as he tried getting even more comfortable. Shruti leaned away and slapped him right across his face.

'What the fuck?' Rahul shouted and tried to catch hold of her hands which she was now swaying wildly in the air.

'Stay away from me, you asshole!' she shouted as he tried to rein her in. The small crowd around their table started looking at them.

'Bitch. Such a slut, you are! You can sleep with that oldie, but not with me. You whore,' he shouted.

'I did *not* sleep with him,' she shouted back and hit him across the face.

'Fuck off. The whole office knows it. He dropped you home once. I saw it. I fucking saw it. And you say you fucking didn't fuck him?'

'NO!'

'You think we are nuts? You used to work late and now you leave office by eight. Do you think we are all fools? Everyone suspected it, bitch. It was a matter of time. The day I told about you in office, your game was over, bitch.'

'You told everyone? YOU?' She opened her eyes and pointed her finger at him. 'I told you that I didn't sleep with him!'

'And you think I will believe a whore like you. I saw you in his car . . .'

At this point, Shruti put her head down and started sobbing.

After a few minutes passed away Rahul placed his hand on her shoulder and said, 'Sorry . . .'

As soon as this happened, she got up and in a very swift motion sent her hand flying to his face getting him in the nose, knocking him down the chair, bleeding profusely from the nose.

Before Rahul knew what hit him, two bouncers, both double his size, walked up to them.

'What is the matter here?'

'She is drunk. Everything is fine,' Rahul said and flashed his best innocent smile. He was desperately trying not to get his teeth knocked in by seven foot giants while clutching at his nose, which was still bleeding. The blow broke his nose bridge.

'I am not drunk. And he is trying to . . .' she said and covered her face and started crying. At this, one bouncer grabbed him by his collar and pulled him up till only his toenails were on the ground.

'Please. I am sorry. She is drunk. She is talking trash. She is a friend of mine. We are very good friends.'

'Are you two friends, ma'am?' The other bouncer asked, his arms crossed on his chest.

'No. Not at all.'

'Oh, yes we are,' Rahul said, with a smile on his battered face.

'Ask him my phone number,' Shruti said to the bouncers.

He did not have it. The bouncers looked at him to see if he had any answer.

After stuttering for a while he answered, 'Umm . . . I have a new phone with me . . . that is why . . .'

'That does not look like a new phone.' A man of authority appeared, of more or less Rahul's age and Shruti didn't catch his face with all the lights flashing behind his head. Probably the manager.

'I can explain . . .' Rahul said.

'Come with us,' the bouncers said and grabbed him by his arm and led him away.

'I can't leave her here,' he said while they were dragging her away.

'She is more safe here than with you, sir,' the guy said and motioned the bouncer to take him away.

This was the last thing he heard before the bouncer punched him unconscious and dumped him outside the back door of the club.

Then they helped Shruti out of her chair and led her to the waiting lounge which accommodated single guests who had blacked out to come back to their senses so that they could be transported home. She was the only one that day. They put her on the couch and she fell asleep.

The manager sat on her side and looked at her. She looked beautiful. And she was mumbling something.

# Of Missing People, Pizzas and Good Looking Men

They called up Shruti's landlord and they informed that she would be home by the next morning.

'Why?' Garima looked at both of them and asked.

Saurav and Abhi were standing at the two corners of the room and she was sitting on the television trolley she had bought for Shruti.

They both looked at her puzzled and checking as to what she meant.

'What?'

'What?'

They both asked.

'I mean this. Why this? You two . . . standing where you are. Shruti . . . god knows where. What did we do wrong to deserve this? Why did we have to go through this? After years, just when I thought things would be alright, it is back to where I started from . . . I trusted you guys with everything. Everything. I so loved you guys . . . and you . . .' She broke down and covered her face. 'I was so lucky I found you. I was so lucky. You made my life so complete. For the first time in years, I felt good about myself. I was so happy and you guys ruined it all. You and you. Maybe me too.' She kept sobbing.

'Everything will be okay,' Abhi said as he came near her.

'Nothing will be alright. Nothing will be alright! What will be alright? You were the one who drove her out. It is because of you that she isn't here. It is you. You started it with Saurav. Why? Why Abhi? I was so happy and for no fault of mine, I am all alone again.'

'You have me.'

'Whatever Abhi . . .'

'Garima . . .' Saurav said for the first time that evening. 'It is my fault too. I was the one who said trash about her . . . to her . . . And I was wrong with Riya too. I should have waited till they had sorted things out.'

'No Saurav . . . I was wrong with that. I should have acted more maturely. I took it a little too far. I should have given you your space. Sorry for that. But you ignored me, man. For her. I mean you should have at least talked to me about it . . . And I thought you would, you know . . . not respect her and . . .' said Abhi.

'I should have asked and talked to you about it. I didn't know what the deal was between the two of you.' Saurav came near and stood near Abhi. 'I was so fucking into her that I forgot about you guys, you, Garima . . . and even Shruti. I don't even remember the last time I talked to her. Damn, I so miss her. I am sorry, Abhi.'

'I am sorry too, Saurav. I screwed it up. I am sorry for whatever I said about you and Riya.'

'It is okay. I incited you to do so.'

'Still, it was me who crossed the line.'

'But I made you do so.'

'But I crossed the line first.'

'What you did was understandable.'

'No dude, it was silly.'

'What I did was silly.'

'I am sorry.'

'I am sorry too.'

They hugged.

Garima broke out in a smile and then burst out, 'So, will you guys now kiss now . . . it looks so . . . it is my mistake honey . . . no, it is mine . . . no, it is mine, sweet heart . . .!' She laughed out loud and rolled over.

All three of them slumped on the ground, on the part which was not soiled up till now. Garima sat between them and put both her hands on their heads which were on her shoulder and she patted them.

'Missing her?' she asked.

'Very much.'

'Never missed anybody like this. It would have been so nice to have her here today,' Saurav said.

'It would have been so nice . . . the four of us . . . on the New Years' eve . . . It would have been ideal . . .' Garima said.

'What?' Saurav asked.

'What?' Abhi asked.

'What what?' Garima said.

'It is . . . Fuck . . . it's 31st?' Saurav said.

'Oh . . . yeah . . . totally skipped,' Abhi added. 'Great. Now I miss her even more.'

The three of them were sitting in a circle and it had been a while since they last sat there. Abhi and Saurav kept talking that day remembering every good thing about Shruti and they didn't seem to run out of them. They were getting overboard with it now that they were even drunk from the left over vodka from the kitchen.

'Yeah man, even in that party . . . the freshers' one . . .? When she wore . . .'

'That red dress . . . superb, man . . . !'

'Superb . . .? Out of the world . . . she is such a hottie, man . . . I miss her . . .'

'I miss seeing her.'

'I miss her smile.'

'I miss her laugh, man . . . the way she . . .'

'I miss her cheeks . . .'

'I miss her breasts . . . I mean I miss her . . . you get the point.'

Garima then pulled his ear and said, 'Abhi? What was I wearing that day?'

'Umm . . . something very nice . . .' he laughed and gave Saurav a high five. 'I do remember. Green dress,' he said and pulled her cheeks.

'What?' Saurav said. 'You should have let her think that you had forgotten!'

'You do that to Riya,' Garima said and everybody stopped talking. The topic had not been raised till the time peace was struck between these two.

'It is okay, guys,' Abhi said. 'I am okay with Riya. Serious.'

The other two were still silent.

He called up Riya.

It had been quite some time that Shruti had been sleeping in the lounge. She had talked a lot last night, and she remembered only pieces of it. She woke up and rubbed her eyes. The place was dead quiet. The place was empty. She would have panicked but her head was being hammered by a million sledgehammers and things were slowly coming back to her.

As soon as she was about to get up, a strong male voice said from behind, 'Sit down.'

She turned around to see a cup in front of her face.

She held the mug and sat from her half standing position.

A man, rather a boy, in his mid-twenties came around and sat in front of her.

'Drink. It will make you feel better.'

'Who are you?' she asked and sipped it. And while doing that she saw that guy.

He seemed to have gotten ready right now. A crisp blue and black striped shirt tucked in a pair of black trousers that ran across his body lines. He got up and the sight of that guy's cute butt made her burn her tongue.

She let out an *oops* and he turned back and said, 'Too hot?'

'Very . . . I mean, yes, it's hot. The coffee. The coffee is hot,' she said and said no further. He was not real. Tall, an olive tanned complexion, and bluish grey eyes that looked to melt her. Not an iota of fat anywhere. The shirt clung to places where there were taut muscles. A face made with a pencil and scale giving him a high jaw line and sharp lines across his face. For a moment she thought she had seen him in a film magazine but then she thought maybe it was just the alcohol from the last night.

Cut off a few years from him and he would look like Tom Cruise from Top Gun, add a few and he would be Clooney from Oceans'.

She left like running her hand through his hair, which was exactly what she always wanted hers to be like. Silky as hell and glossy like anything glossy. He stood in front of her and waited for her to finish the coffee. She kept drinking it as it was a glass of milk with her mother, and not the stunning Adonis, standing over her. She stole a few glances at him. She so wanted to cling to him. His strong arms around her and looking into his eyes.

Shruti could not get his hair out of her mind. She even started envying it. They were long and ended just above where his ears ended and slightly flopped over on eye.

'Are you okay?' he asked and unbuttoned his sleeves.

'Hmm.' She thought saying a yes would mean leaving that place.

'Long night, eh?' he said as he rolled up his sleeves. Shruti thought that if that's how he looked after a long night, what he would look like after a shower. Or *in* the shower. She had started imagining herself to be in it, when the urgency of the situation shook her in.

'Yes. Who are you?' she asked.

'Me? I work here.'

'Where is he?'

'Rahul? We sent him home. He wasn't in his best behaviour last night.'

'I know.' Shruti was already losing it in his voice. 'Did I do something stupid yesterday?'

'Not really. You just broke Rahul's nose.'

'Shit. Did I say something stupid?'

'You said a lot of things. Mostly non-stupid. I can try a hand at writing you your biography.'

'Shit,' she said and covered her mouth.

'It's all cool. I had an interesting night. Tell me when you are ready. I will be behind that door. Anything you need, call from that phone,' he said and pointed to a phone and got up.

Shruti wanted to pull him down and hug him and go to sleep. Forever.

But she kept sitting there looking at him till the time she realized that her mouth was half open and a stream of saliva was threatening to come down.

He smiled and walked away.

She flopped back on the couch, grabbed a pillow and hugged it real tight.

Images came back from last night when she had done so last night, hugged him and told him whatever had happened with her. All of it. In long winding sentences.

She saw him disappear behind the doors which had the placard with MANAGER embellished on it.

It took a frantic Shruti ten minutes and a bag full of cosmetics to come out all shining and fresh, as if woken up from an eight hour sleep.

She sat on the couch and held her head between her hands and thought about the sentences she had told herself last night.

*I am not going back to them.*

*It is my life. My happiness. I am not going back to Delhi.*

She would find somebody who could take care of both of them, somebody who could take her out of her misery. Anybody.

She wiped off the beads of tears and felt good about herself. Liberated.

Ten minutes passed by before she thought she would finally knock on his door. Manager.

She took a deep breath and knocked on his door.

'Come in,' he called from inside.

She entered. 'Hi.'

'Oh! You are looking . . . fresh,' he said as he slapped down his laptop and looked at her.

'Thank you.'

He was almost exactly what she had imagined last night. Smart. Young. Handsome. And probably rich. Trying to get rich on her own steam didn't work out too well, so this was the only way out.

'Where do I drop you?'

'Hmmm . . .?' The word *home* skipped her tongue, a touch of sadness came across her face and she looked down.

'Why should we not have breakfast first?' He got up and walked up to her. 'Shall we?'

'Sure,' she said, half lost in his thoughts.

'You okay?'

'Yeah,' she said and they walked out of the room.

He walked down the stairs and took her hand, believing that she was still not in a good shape. She wasn't, but the reason wasn't the hangover. It was him.

His hand felt like a thousand feathers on her hand, only that they were strong and could have snapped her fingers into two.

They walked to his car. They passed a few small ones and a few big ones to reach a really big one.

What the fuck, Shruti eyes said as he beeped open the car.

It was a Porsche, a Gleaming blue convertible. Just like the one she had dreamed of owning when she would be twice her age.

She was still standing there waiting to make sure that it was actually the car she had to get into when he opened the door and swished his hand motioning her to sit.

Shruti's heart skipped a few more beats. It was like a fairy tale come true. Like a morning wish. She wouldn't let him go, she had decided.

Losing her job in an impulse was enough for a lifetime.

He backed the car out of the driveway and drove like only stunt drivers could. Had she seen anybody drive like that, she would have called her a maniac. But he was driving well, whatever his name was. And that he was cute and smelled like heaven helped too.

'I am Rishab.'

'I am Shruti.'

'So Shruti, where do you work?' he looked at her and asked.

'Silverman Finance. Not anymore.' Her mood took a dip.

'Silverman Finance. Hmm . . . I knew that you had resigned but not that it was Silverman. Anyway, feeling any better from last night?'

'Yup.' Shruti now was really falling for this guy. She was just waiting for the guy to confirm the car was his own. She would really fall for him then, in deep love and never to recover.

'Nice car,' Shruti said as she thought every guy likes his car to be praised.

'Thank you. A few perks when you are born a little rich,' he said disdainfully.

'Don't say that. You seem to be doing well. Manager of the Elan. That is good, isn't it?'

'I own that place.'

'What?' She couldn't keep this one in.

'Yes.'

'That is so strange? Then why are you acting chauffeur to drunken guests like me? I mean . . . '

The car suddenly seemed in place. There would a few more in his garage. And she smiled at the fact.

'Tonight is the 31st night bash so I thought I would give my people a break. And moreover, it doesn't hurt to have a beautiful girl by your side on a breakfast table, does it?'

Her cheeks went red and hot, she sank in her seat melted away and became the seat cushions. 'Probably, yes. Thank you,' she said, all flushed. She wanted to be in love again and she was trying hard on this one. *The hot rich one*. She was glad she was doing well.

'Where would you like to have your breakfast, Shruti?' he asked.

'Wherever you want to.'

'I will make it easier for you. I will drive past a few eating places. Choose the one you like.'

'Okay.'

He was yet to drive along the first eating joint when Shruti shrieked out.

'That one.'

And then looked the other way as if it was a mistake.

'Which one?'

'Nothing.'

'You mean that?'

'Umm . . . yes . . . but it is no compulsion.'

She had pointed to a small roadside *dhaba* that the four of them used to go to after office. They were the first one to come by that day. Shruti was really embarrassed to choose that one.

A boy of fourteen came to their table as soon as they settled down and said, 'Rishab *bhaiya, kya loge aaj*?'

Shruti looked at him with a shocked expression on her face.

'Not my first time. You see, every other eating joint in the city is competition. So I like this place!'

She laughed.

'Hi. Riya?'

'Yes. Who is this?' she asked.

'Abhi.'

'Hi Abhi. How are you? It is so nice . . . .'

'Yes, Riya . . . are you free right now? Have you seen Shruti's place? We want you to come there. Can you? Will you?'

'Yes, I have . . . but why?'

'Just come here. Okay? See you in twenty minutes,' he said and put down the phone.

Garima and Saurav looked at each other and laughed.

'What? What?' he kept asking them for the next five minutes and they kept laughing!

It was well half an hour after that Abhi got back in to his senses and realized what he was up to.

'I knew what I was doing, people. I know I was drunk, but I also knew what I was doing. But she should have been here by now? Isn't it?'

'Yes. I guess so. Must be on her way. Anyway. I need to eat something.'

'Yeah, yeah,' Garima said. 'I have an idea. Let's decorate

this place! What say? A sorry, plus a New Year party? And then we will call every one over and have a big bash?'

'Everyone?' Abhi asked.

'I mean Deb and Avantika. Sameer?'

'Then we will need more food, won't we?' Saurav asked.

'Fine by me,' Abhi said.

'But then, when do we order the food and stuff?'

'We'll need five pizzas,' Garima said.

'Okay then, ten pizzas on the way,' he said and flicked up his car keys and barged through the door before anybody could say anything, leaving Garima and Abhi smiling at each other.

'We need to get the house in place,' Garima said with both her hand on her waist and let out a deep sigh and stared at Abhi.

'Don't tell me you want me to get all this cleaned up.'

'As a matter of fact I do.'

'*Arey,* we will do it *together*. What will *you* do if I do this?'

'We need to decorate this place. Balloons and all that. I will go get those.'

'Please let me go. You will have to walk so far to get that.'

'As if you care!'

'I do! Please let me go.'

'Shut up. And by the time I come this should be clean,' she said and left.

He looked at the floor and looked heavenwards.

They had ordered more than their fill that day.

Hot *laccha paranthas* with buckets full of *dal makhani* and *shahi paneer*.

'Now that's real food,' Rishab said and dug in.

The plates were licked clean in a matter of minutes.

'*Ab bas*, I need my bed and a warm quilt and doze off! Brilliant start to a great day.'

'True,' she said with a bit of sadness in her voice which Rishab was quick to catch.

'Unless, of course . . . Ms Shruti . . .' He leant forward. '. . . has some other plans?'

'Other plans? No,' she said. 'You have had a long day, you really need to sleep. Thank you for this. But I can't take more of your time.'

'You are not taking my time. I am wilfully offering you mine! Shall we?' He thrust out his hand to pull her out of her chair.

'Rishab, I think I need to go now,' she said.

'Why? Somebody waiting?'

'No, but . . .'

'Then shut up. Want to catch a movie?'

'I don't know . . . New York?'

'Okay, New York!' he said. 'Will you drive?'

'I can't drive! Not that thing.'

'Have a license?'

'Yes . . . but . . .'

'Here.' He threw the keys to her.

She looked at keys and the four buttons on it all of which seemed equally capable of opening the car. She pressed one and nothing happened. She pressed all and the car opened.

They got in.

'These things are a little funny,' he chuckled.

'Shut up. Whatever happened to insert and open?'

'That can have many connotations, actually?'

'Dirty mind.'

'Thank you.'

'Whatever.'

'Ha!'

She tuned the key and gave it too much.

Rishab cringed and then smiled.

'I am sorry,' she said and smiled. 'I told you I can't drive this.'

'You can.'

'Oh hell, I am used to driving Porsche's with someone like you sitting next to me.'

'Excuse me?'

'Nothing. Just shut up,' she said.

Rishab smiled.

'And anyway if I bang this thing in to anything you know I can't afford even a head light of this. So it your loss.'

'Dad's.'

The first try was a horrendous one. But thereafter she did better. Changing gears on time and driving smoothly. A feather touch and the car was already doing eighty.

'Take a left from there,' he pointed.

'Rishab, you want to watch it for sure?'

'You chose the movie. Why? You don't?'

'No I mean I can drive this for three hours. You go and watch the movie,' she laughed.

'You seriously want to?'

'I mean I can. It is probably the first time, and the last time I am sitting in a car like this.'

'Good for me, that you like driving it.'

'Why so?'

'I always dreamed of date, where my girl would drive!'

'Your girl?' she said with a scorn. That is another matter that her brain erased everything else to accommodate this memory of hers and several copies of it.

'Umm . . . I mean, the girl with me . . .'. For the first time, he fumbled with words.

'Date?'

'Yes . . . that is true. It is a date, isn't it?'

'Okay, I will give that one to you.'

'Good.'

'One question.'

'Shoot,' He said and pointed to a direction that lead to a highway. She was cruising at ninety kilometres an hour now.

'How many *my girls* have been there?'

'Hmm . . . you wouldn't want to know.'

'Okay,' She clenched the steering wheel in anger.

'But you are the first on to drive my car!'

'Thanks for the privilege,' she said wryly.

'You are welcome. But tell me? Are you jealous?'

'Why would I be?'

'Maybe you have started liking me?' he said, smiled and looked at her.

She wanted to thrust her head out from the sun roof and shout that out to the world and flaunt her guy around. 'Not at all.'

'Then why are you with me right now?' He smiled again.

'First, I am jobless. Second, I have nothing to do. And third, I am hoping to use you to get myself a job somewhere!'

'How mean, Shruti.'

'That is how I am,' she said and shrugged her shoulders.

'I like you the way you are.'

'Are you flirting with me?'

'Depends. Is it working?' he asked.

'No.'

'Then, I am not.'

'You know what; I have heard these dialogues from somewhere,' he said.

'Get Smart, the movie.'

'You have seen that movie?' she asked.

'I watch every movie that comes out.'

'Why did you miss that movie then?'

'I have seen it.'

'But it released today.'

'Special screening. John Abraham and friends.' He looked at her and smiled and asked her to drive on.

It was a tough job indeed.

Abhi had his gloves on taken from the Shruti's hair cover box. Two handkerchiefs on his mouth and nose. He wished he could have one on his eyes too.

He nearly puked twice while scraping off the dried portions of the puke. He started hating Shruti and alcohol with every passing moment. Just as he was done pouring water over the floor for the umpteenth time that morning there was a knock on the door.

You might have guessed it right.

It was Riya.

He opened the door thinking it would be Garima and thrust

his smelly hands out and shouted form beneath his handkerchiefs, 'Smell this!'

Riya dodged his outstretched hands and that's when he saw it was not her.

'Hi,' he said.

'What?' she said.

'Hi Riya,' he said before he realized that his voice was getting muffled beneath the handkerchiefs. He took them off.

'Hi Abhi.'

'Hi. Long time. Sit, sit. I am sorry for the mess. Actually it isn't mine. I am just cleaning it up.'

'Need help?'

'Sure do,' he said and she gave him the same beamer that she used to give him during their colleges days.

'You look cool with those handkerchiefs on your face. Can I get one too . . . the colour suits you . . . I had that handkerchief . . . the pooh ones . . . really cute and guess what . . . they were on sale . . . Cool, huh?'

'That is indeed nice. There.' He passed on one to her.

She put on the handkerchief and said, 'Now we are ready.' She took a wiper in hand. 'Let's do some cleaning!' She smiled, showing all thirty two.

Together they took well over half an hour to make that place shine as it never had before. They wiped the floor clean till it shone and they dusted the home till it shone too!

'Here. Come, let's take a picture,' Riya said once they were over. She put her cell phone on self-timer and put in on the television and they both stood side by side with handkerchiefs on their heads and mouths and wipers in hand.

'Not like this. No!' Riya shouted as soon as the first picture got clicked.

She set the camera on the self-timer again and came and positioned Abhi and herself in a pose. Then came a million different poses and a zillion more pictures.

They were exhausted from the running from the camera and aligning themselves in a particular pose in the mere ten second that they had. Riya was never satisfied with one take. She took five of each at least, much to Abhi's frustration.

They sat down on the bed that they had now rolled out and had spread out a nice blue bed sheet on.

They exchanged nothing for the next two minutes, just caught hold of their breath and smiled at whatever had just happened in last one hour. The other two were not there yet.

'Riya. I am sorry. I know I have said a lot of not so nice things about you to Saurav. But I am sorry. Really sorry.'

'So finally,' she said and rubbed her palms together. Then, she smiled wickedly, 'The stubborn creature realizes his mistake!'

'That is rude.'

'Yes, I know. I am sorry. I should have understood you back then. But seriously, I really liked you and loved you as a friend. You were the only perfect part of my life back then. And once you went . . . everything fell apart. The movies, the dance . . . everything became history. I turned into you. Books, professors, assignments . . . I don't know why . . . I so wanted you to be around during those days . . . but . . .' She now had tears in her eyes. 'And yes, you were right . . . he left me . . . no prizes for guessing that . . . ' she said and smiled a little.

'Good for you.'

'And see, I am almost where you are! You should be proud of yourself. It is probably because of you that I am here,' she said. Her tone alternated between a sad and a sprightly one.

Her eyes had started to get wet when Abhi got up and took

her in his arms and then she started crying a little more . . . before crying a lot more.

They stood there for quite some time, before she broke out of his embrace and looked at him with her cutest smile and tears in the her eyes and said, 'You were my best friend, you are my best friend, and you will always be! Whether you like it or not.' She broke out of his hug completely and said, 'I will show you something.'

'What it is?' he asked.

'Just wait,' she said and started looking for her handbag around the house.

She got hold of it and rummaged through it. She took out something out and walked close to Abhi.

'Something I had kept for posterity . . . for this day . . . and the days that we will celebrate our friendship,' she said and kept three stapled clutches of pages on the table and said.

'Assignments . . . that is law . . . and . . . ' she said.

' . . . macro,' he said.

'And economics.'

They hugged. They looked each in the eye and Abhi said, 'Missed you.'

'Missed you too.'

'I love you so much.'

'I love you too.'

They came close and her lips touched his, they kissed for a few split seconds before realizing what they'd done and they parted.

'I am sorry,' he said.

'I am sorry too.'

They looked into each other eyes. He pulled her into himself and kissed her deep. She kissed him back deeply. Kissed like lovers. Kissed to make up for the time they weren't together.

'Between the two of us?' he asked.

'Forever.'

'You know John Abraham? You do?'

'Yes. Why? You like him?'

'Hmm . . . not that much. But I think you are too rich to understand that meeting superstars is a big thing. I have friends who show their pictures with Shahrukh and Aamir when they were three years old . . .' she mocked

'Okay, okay!'

'Whatever,' she said.

'See that is why I hate being what I am.'

'Why?' she asked.

'I say things or do things and people think I am arrogant. I have not lived your life and I don't know and I am not expected to know. Maybe I have got everything in life but there is a possibility that I might have earned it too.'

'Elaborate.'

'I could be as good as you are. If I were in your place I might have got where you are. Getting in Silverman Finance is a big deal and I know that. But I might have been that good. Maybe I am. But just because I have every comfort in the world and was born with a silver spoon in my mouth that doesn't mean people won't ever give me credit for whatever I do. They will have just one thing to say. *Dad's money making the way for the son.* And believe me, hearing that is way worse than not getting clicked with superstars,' he said and looked away.

'Yes. That is true. But I wonder sometimes why you people never go to Indian colleges. You still choose the easy path. I have a friend who is quite rich may not be as rich as you are but he is an IITian. Why not you?'

'Saurav?'

'Yes,' she said.

He remembered it from the last night blabbering of Shruti.

'See Shruti. When you have pots of dad's money lying around you wouldn't like to be a speck in the engineer world. And when you see that kind of money the only thing that gets drilled in your mind by your family is to think how to make more out of it. This guy you are talking about, what do his parents do?'

'Engineer and Doctor.'

'See my point. It is how you are bred,' he continued with authority dripping from his voice. 'When I was twenty, I dropped out of business school for this project and I have been toiling hard. Yes, I don't have to catch buses and autos but I am working. And hard enough. I know this night club thing might seem like something too frivolous a thing to start your business with. Something like, oh, it's like a rich man's wife doing an interior designers' course. But let me tell you, it is not easy. My point is—I am rich, that is not my fault. It has been two years and this place will break even in four. That is success. For me, at least. People may attribute it to my dad, but I will fiercely defend it as mine,' he said and looked ahead.

'Point taken,' she said. And she had done a calculation. He was twenty two!

Her luck was changing. And changing fast.

They drove on the highway for a little while after which she got a little bored and asked, 'What next? I am getting a little bored.'

'Oh, are you? Want to feel a rush?'

'Umm . . . yes . . .' she said sceptically. 'What do you have in mind?'

'Ever raced a plane?'

'What? Do I look like I might have done it?'

'Want to do it?'

'Are you drunk?'

'No.'

'Are you kidding me?'

'No.'

'Are you nuts?'

'A little bit. Maybe.'

'Okay. You do it as I am none of the above. I will watch.'

'Okay.'

'Are you serious?' she asked now. She had thought he was kidding.

'Hell, yeah.'

They stopped and switched their seats and they drove on to the highway. He nodded at the person who was there at what looked like a runway and he let them through the guarded barricade.

They stopped there for a while.

'Look,' he showed a small jet approaching the runway in his back mirror.

'Oh shit. You are really gonna race that?'

'Seems like . . . Yes!'

'Umm . . .'

'What?'

'Don't do it.'

'Why?'

'Umm . . .'

'Scared?'

'A little.'

'Good.'

He pushed on the gas and the car was surrounded by white smoke and burnt rubber.

The jet was a kilometre away when it shattered the glasses of the shiny blue Porsche and made it seem like a small toy.

Rishab clenched the wheel and let the brakes go.

First second. 20 km /hr.

Second. 69km/hr.

Third. 92km/hr.

They both hit the back of their seats. Any faster and they would have broken their necks.

The car was moving fast now. The road was getting blurred. The car had started shaking. They were surrounded in car smoke.

Fourth second. 145 km/hr.

The car was racing now. A few more seconds and the beast reached 135 when the jet crossed them overhead making the car a bit unsettled. Rishab pushed on the gas further.

He was going 190.

One rock and the car would have smashed to pieces.

'Stop it! Oh shit! Are you . . .?' Shruti wanted to shout out but her voice failed. She closed her eyes and grabbed on to the sides of the seat. Her stomach was churning five times as much as they do on roller coaster rides.

The car had started to vibrate wildly, seeming it would topple over. They had both been pushed to the seat and they could feel the air fighting them.

The sights had gone. They could see just two colours—blue of the sky and a blurred brown road ahead.

The jet had was slowing down and was about to touch down.

He gave the car its last and pushed on the pedal.

It touched 250 km/hr. and the jet touched down. They were flying. She felt weightless.

He raced past it.

He won. By the nose, but won.

Rishab waved at the pilot and the pilot gave him a thumbs-up.

They just came to a stop and he took the last bit out of the tires by doing a 360 degree donut turn a few yards in front of the jet. It nearly made Shruti puke.

'It is over,' he whispered in her ear. She opened her eyes, still in a daze. She rushed out of the car and slammed the door. She bent down with her palms against the knees and was panting.

Rishab came out and said, 'I am sorry, but I couldn't have stopped midway. And by the way, I won.'

He thought she would puke too. There had been guys who had puked.

'Are you okay?' he asked and bent down.

She looked at him, still bent, 'Can we do it again?'

'But you closed your eyes.'

'Obviously, I closed my eyes! This was my first time! But now I regret it. It was so good,' she said and held him by his arm.

'I know.'

They kept standing there looking back at the runway and the barren lands they had whizzed past. It was quite a distance and took just a few seconds.

'I think I now have to thank you for a lot of things,' she said.

'Don't mention it. '

'No, I really have to.'

'If you just have to, treat me.'

'I will, someday.'

'Today.'

'Today? I think you should rest. We should really be going home now. It is 31st today and a big day for your club. We should be going now.'

'Oh! Big business woman, you are! Shut up!'

'So, where are we going?'

'Are you serious?'

'Do I look like I am laughing?'

'Okay, then. You choose. I will drive and you point on where you want to eat.'

'I have kind of decided. It is Palates of the World.'

'Perfect. Can I drive?'

'Yes. You can.'

'Fine.'

'But there is a slight problem.'

'What?'

'I don't think you have a license.'

'Oh, yes I do!'

'No you don't.'

'What?'

'The restaurant is in Delhi.'

'What?'

'We are flying.'

He turned her around and pointed to the jet standing there.

She fainted.

'Did we interrupt?' Saurav came in with a host of pizzas and a few bottles of coke. Abhi was hugging Riya when he came in.

Along with him came Garima and both of them smiled seeing them together. A few minutes before and they would have caught them kissing.

All of them hugged in pairs. All the six possibilities in varying degrees of tears in their eyes.

'Have heard a lot about you,' Garima said to Riya.

'I hope it is more good than bad,' Riya chuckled. 'And you have the most beautiful eyes ever. Ever. Trust me. And those earrings you wore that day . . . I just love them . . . Where did you get them from . . . ? By the way, we cleaned up the house . . . '

And clean it was.

Garima and Saurav were duly impressed by the work these two had done for the house.

They sat down and started talking.

They all said they missed Shruti. They had called her landlord more than a few times, but she said that Shruti was out and that she would back to her place by this night.

All four of them started working on the balloons and the charts.

Huge ones.

One which said—**Happy New Year**

And the second one said—**We are Sorry**

Both charts were half the size of each wall and were in blazing red on a white background. Tubes of sparkling stuff were emptied over the charts.

Satisfied with what they had done, they hauled up the charts on the walls and nailed them in.

They went on to plaster the other walls with frills, Christmas balls and stars till the whole room was glittering.

They had gone a little overboard with everything.

Tired as hell, they went to sleep.

Not before Saurav ordered two four pound cakes and two more pizzas, two crates of beer, three vodka bottles and ten bottles of Sprite.

Last extravagance, Saurav told himself. All of them were sure to lose their jobs. But that day wasn't the one they would think about that.

Rishab helped Shruti on to the stairs to the jet where a man in a butler's and two men in pilot's uniforms were waiting to greet them.

'Good morning, Shruti,' the pilots echoed.

'Good morning ma'am,' the butler said as he handed out towels to both of them.

Rishab led her to main sitting area.

'How do they know my name?'

'Technology has come a long way sweet heart,' he whispered.

They finally sat down in two huge black sized lazy boy chairs and the butler/waiter served them water after which Rishab asked him to leave them alone for a while.

'One question, Rishab. Just one question.'

'Shoot.'

'Just exactly how much money does your dad have?' she said and stared.

He laughed. 'Hmm . . . we have three of these.'

'You must be having it tough making your ends meet Rishab. Only three?'

'Yes,' he chuckled.

She sat back up in her seat and asked, 'Are you mentally retarded?'

'Why? Why are you saying that?'

'No. seriously. Where is that butler, I should ask him.'

'Why?'

'Why? Why all this? I mean why *me*? Why not some starlet? Model? Anyone? Why me? And why all this?'

'What all this?'

'All this? I have never seen the inside of a Porsche. Or a jet. And I have never seen you before. Why all this? Is this even for real?'

'Hmmm . . . let's just say, you are very special.'

'Not convincing enough.' She kicked back and drifted away. There was a slight fear in her mind that he may be doing it just because he needed a nice new girl to lay. But the Porsche ride and the little chance that she might end up being with him was good enough for the risk taken.

A loud rumbling of the plane shook her and she got up. She was tightly strapped and safe. Not to forget tucked in neatly by Rishab in a nice warm blanket.

'Delhi.'

'Are you for real or should I go back to sleep?' she asked groggily with a smile.

'Very real.' He got up and pecked her on her cheek. 'Let's go.'

He turned around and Shruti sat there with a hand on her cheek and eyes wide open, too shocked to believe what had just happened. Not just what happened a second ago, but what was happening since morning. The day before, she lay sloshed in her apartment with no one to call her own and now she was in Delhi, with this mysteriously good looking and awesomely rich guy, sitting in his jet on New Year's Eve.

'Let's go,' he now said in a louder tone.

'Yes, sure. Let us go. No problem,' she mocked. 'I was in Hyderabad this morning and I am in Delhi now . . . No problem whatsoever . . .' her voice trailed off as she got up.

They drove on in the beast of a car, an SLR Mercedes Convertible and reached Greater Kailash where he had picked out the restaurant.

The door keeper knew her name too. She gave the same bewildered look to him.

They went inside and the place and the she thought would be brimming with people was empty.

Instead, a huge banner had the words **WELCOME SHRUTI** written on it.

Right in front of them!

She looked at him and he looked back and smiled. Shocks had become the order of the day.

They sat down at a corner and the pianist started belting out some really great sounding tunes.

'I miss them,' she said. A tear rolled off her pretty face and wetted the napkin below.

'Everything is going to all right. We will talk to them once we are in Hyderabad.'

'*We?*'

'I mean if you want me to, I can talk to them.' He came to sit next to her. He took her hands into his and looked at her.

'Are we meeting again?' she looked at him teary eyed.

'Had my mother been alive I would have had her meet you. Does that feel like we are meeting again?'

'No, I just thought . . . I am sorry. I don't know. You are good looking . . .'

'Am I?' he asked and smiled.

'You know you are . . . you have all this . . .' She pointed to the restaurant.

'This is not mine . . . rented . . . '

'Not my point! You are rich, good looking, smart and everything. And most importantly, you don't know me. Why all this, Rishab?'

'Do you think that after last night I don't know you?'

'Did I sleep with you?'

'NO! You didn't! But you talked a lot. And I feel I know you for years.'

'Please don't show me dreams that . . .'

'I wouldn't . . . This is not a dream.'

They sat there hand in hand till it was late evening.

It was ten at night when the four of them finally woke up, ten minutes after the incessant ringing of the bell by the delivery guys.

They took the delivery and sat in a circle. They rubbed their eyes and yawned, none of them in any mood to party that night. Shruti was still untraceable. The house was still decorated as such, only that the posters had moved down from one of the corners and nobody was interested enough to set it right.

They had slept well and they wanted to sleep more.

Saurav pulled out another mattress from the bed room and a couple of quilts and they all got inside it. They loved it now.

The couples hugged and lay there exchanging sweet nothings and telling each other how lucky they were to have each other in their lives. They had now realized how futile it was to have a great party.

It doesn't matter where you are on the New Year's Eve. A big club. A great party. Nothing matters. It is with who you are on that day.

At the back of their minds, they were thinking of Shruti, who was somewhere out there with somebody they didn't know. They were terribly worried about her. More than that, they were slightly jealous because she was doing fine and she didn't need them to be near for even the New Year. They wanted her back. They wanted things to be as they were. They wanted their group to be complete again.

They had boarded the plane just before 10:00 p.m.

Shruti had pestered him to go back to Hyderabad before it struck 12 and be there at his night club that night.

All his fervent requests were turned down and he was categorically told to shut up till the time they reached the club.

They reached Hyderabad and rushed to the club. Rishab drove like a maniac as he had sworn on her that he wouldn't say a thing before they reached the club and it was getting mighty difficult for him to do so.

Rishab pecked her once or twice when they stopped at red lights. She made a purring sound every time and went back to sleep.

'I had a great time today,' Rishab said as they stood outside the back entrance of Elan. 'You know what?' Rishab said started walking away. 'I don't care about the party anymore. You do. So, go ahead attend it.'

'*What?* I don't own this place. Rishab! Are you out of your mind?'

'No. Come with me, I will show you something,' he said and started rushing towards the road and waited for Shruti to come.

'What the . . .'

They crossed the road and reached the other side where there was a half built apartment. It's construction seemed to have been stopped long back.

'Where are we going?' Shruti asked as Rishab led her into darkness.

They crossed the half broken rusted brown gate of the apartment. There were mounds of hardened cement and sand everywhere and stray dogs had made this place their haven. It was pitch-dark. There were truck trails everywhere with a broken down truck lying upside down at a distance. It looked like it had been years since anyone had been there. There were no traces of human existence. Barring the croaking of crickets, there was an eerie silence all around them.

'Just come.' He clutched her hand again and they jumped on the mounds and entered what would have been the lobby of the building.

They reached the bottom of the flight of the stairs which went up twenty three stories and they could see the moonlight coming in through the terrace of the building.

'Where?' she asked.

'Up there,' he pointed upwards.

Before she could say anything, he had already started going up the stairs and was pulling her up with him. They went on climbing the stairs, Rishab out of instinct and Shruti following him step for step.

They had climbed five stories now and the darkness engulfed them.

Shruti had started panting and it was all too evident.

Without asking for permission, he turned around and pulled her near himself. In one fluid motion, he swept her feet off the ground and picked her up. She was off the ground now, with one arm around his neck and one around it, clutching the first one. She wanted to scream out as she looked down the stairs which had no railing but she felt safe in his arms as he strode up the stairs as if she weighed nothing. She kept her head close to his chest. She felt like losing herself in him. She already had.

'I can walk,' she murmured half-heartedly.

'I know,' he said and kept walking up. He had a strong grip around her and his legs did not miss a pace.

Shruti thought if she was ever to fall in love again, it would be now. Perfect catch, she said to herself.

Rishab kept pace and never slacked as he walked up floor after floor. They got nearer to the light. Shruti looked down once and her stomach churned.

They reached the twenty third floor of what was planned to be the terrace of that building.

'See,' he said and pointed out in the direction of the club.

She saw the place beautifully lit up in all kinds of lights. She could not hear a thing but she could feel the beats of the music thump against the windows of the club.

She looked around to see the entire Hyderabad city was lit up. It was full of activity, there were cars buzzing around, buses, autos, all looking like specks from up there. They were far removed from the chaos, the rush and the revelry.

He went to the edge of the building and sat with his legs dangling down from there. Shruti was looking at him from distance, too scared to say anything.

'Rishab, come back from there,' she said. The terrace had no railing and it scared the shit out of her.

He didn't reply. He looked back and motioned her to come near. With trembling feet and hands, she gave her hand to him and sat down at a little distance, at the edge of the building. She looked down almost thirty stories. Her heart pounded as Rishab pulled her close as she clutched on to him with all her life. They were sitting with nothing under their feet but a dark twenty storey drop. She looked down, her stomach felt strange and she hung on to him harder.

'This is my favourite place ever since I was twelve.' He looked at her and held her hand in his. He looked at those hands and started to caress them.

He continued, 'This was to be built in my mother's name. It was my mother's dream. She wanted this to be an office that would be the nerve centre of all the school and colleges she wanted to open for the poor. She wanted her office to be right here, where we are sitting. My father thought it was a waste of money. Mom had never asked for anything in life except this. He could well afford it. But he couldn't see his money not making more money. He thought my mother wanted this because she had nothing to do. Once she died, this never got completed . . . He never got time from sleeping with female starlets who were younger than I was.' He stopped and few tears hit her hands. He collected himself, started staring at a distance and continued, 'He wanted to convert this in to an upscale residential apartment. The government didn't allow that and he stopped the investment. He blocked all funds. I talked to him and he said business can't be compromised for dead people's dreams,' he said and paused.

'He tried to sell it off but nobody would take it. When I was twenty, I overheard my dad talking to somebody who was ready to buy it. That is why, Shruti, I am not a graduate. It was the tough way out. I came here and asked my father to give me that. He funded that. Elan. That loud, terrible place needed more money than this. We had to bribe the whole state for it. But my father didn't mind. I told him this place would be a huge resident hotel someday. He didn't sell it. Yes, it will be the way mom wanted it. This is what my dream is,' he said. 'Not that.' He pointed to the club.

He wasn't crying anymore. They were quiet for a while. Shruti didn't say a word. She didn't have anything to say.

'I have never talked to anyone about it . . . and I don't know why I told you this. But something happened last night . . . I mean, the way you talked to me . . . it felt good. I didn't want to let you go . . . Something didn't let me leave you today. And trust me you are not the first drunk beautiful girl that I have met.'

'Okay,' she said with a frown.

'I mean, yes . . . As in, you are the most beautiful of them . . . and the most charming one too . . . When I saw you last night, I don't know . . . I couldn't move an inch. I sat there the whole night, just looking at you as you spoke, cried, balled up and slept so peacefully. I envied you. I wanted that calm. I know all this is not making sense at all, but I totally got hooked. I wished the night would last forever. I don't know what love is, I don't want to know what it is, and I don't know whether it is this. All I know is that I wished you wouldn't blow me off this morning. All I wished was that I could talk to you once. All I wanted was for you to stay with me. Deep inside, I wished it would go as it going right now.' He put his hand out and she put hers into his. He pulled her near and hugged her.

He slipped his hand into his pocket and put on a slow English number that Shruti didn't recognize but it was good enough to slow dance on, especially with her head against his shoulder.

'Shruti, that is a dream that fades. You are a dream that I hope never will. I never wish to wake up, if it is one. I don't know what this is, but whatever it is, I sure like it. I sure like you. And I sure like *us*. The first smile you gave this morning, it is still here, I remember those lips curving to give your face that glow that is still lightening up my life. I know it sounds crazy, but if I have ever felt . . . ever, *ever* felt that there is something to really live for and live by for the rest of this life, it is today. I don't know where we go from here, I don't know what will happen from here, but whatever happens, this day will be my most cherished one. You will be my most cherished person.'

'But . . . why me?' she asked as she looked up from her embrace, still teary eyed.

'I don't have an answer.'

He looked at her staring at him, clutched her tighter and moved his head close to her.

'What I do know is this is my best new year ever.' He bent over and she closed her eyes. She waited to be kissed.

He looked at her face gleaming under the moonlight. The wind made her hair fall on her face; he stroked her hair and tucked them behind her ear, not letting her move. He closed his eyes and moved his head closer to hers. She could feel his breath and her pulse racing. He bent down to her face, his lips touched hers.

Fireworks went off, coming through the unfinished roof off the Elan, filling up the sky in blue and red lights, while they kissed. Her lips firmly enveloped in his and his in hers, their tongues twirled each other's around while the embrace got stronger. Shruti hung on to him with curled toes as Rishab slipped her shirt off her shoulder and kissed her. Her hands started working on his shirt, unbuttoning it. She lost her footing and Rishab grabbed her to bring her back from the edge.

His hands slipped in and moved up her back. She clawed in as she cringed and bit his shoulder. She climbed on to him as his hands gripped her and slipped the shirt off her.

'Rishab . . .'

'What?'

'Take this off . . .' She pulled at his vest.

'Not fair.' He tugged at her bra.

'Don't even think . . . '

'Try me.' He put her on the ground, gripped her close and turned her around. He unhooked her.

'Oh . . .' she said as she turned around and hugged him, her breasts crushing against his chest, her nails clawing on his back.

'Now it is fair.' He pushed her against a beam.

'It's not.' She pushed him away and pulled his belt off him.

'It will be.' He charged in and pinned her hands against the beam with one of his. The other one was on her jeans.

'You are not . . .' she shouted and dug her teeth on his chest till he screamed out.

She was naked now. Only her chocolate skin and a smirk.

'Now what?' She whispered in her ear, licking it.

'You will know . . . ' He kissed her as his hands ran on her naked smooth skin.

They fought. They bit. They clawed.

Fireworks lit up the sky.

New Year's Eve came and went and the four of them kept lying there.

The vodka had already been opened and so had the beers. Since they had realized nobody was coming home, they took it on themselves to see to it that not a drop of it was wasted.

Not even a single drop was wasted. They were.

They were totally sloshed. Nobody knew when the year changed its last digit!

They took turns to use the washroom and puke their guts out.

Soon afterwards, they all lay down and dozed off.

# Real Good

It was three in the night when Saurav's phone rang in Shruti's bedroom.

'What?' Riya got up and asked sleepily.

'I will get it.' Saurav kissed her and got up to get the phone. He hoped it was Shruti.

He came back and slept next to her after he kept down the phone.

'Who was it?'

'Nobody,' he said as he hugged her.

'What did nobody say?' She kissed him as she pulled the quilt over both of them.

'Nobody said that all of us are very smart and we deserve to be happy.' He hugged her and they slept off.

This was the conversation that happened in the next room.

'Hello? Is that Saurav?'

'Yes, who is this?'

'Rajat Thapar.'

'Yes, sir! Happy New Year. How can—'

'Cut the dung. What do you think you will do?' Thapar was frantic. He was calm by other people standards, but frantic by his.

'I don't get it.'

Rajat had been looking at the tapes of the video he had accumulated over the last six months.

'*I don't get it?* You son of a bitch. I just went through the security tapes and I saw what you did that day. You think you can keep your job by blackmailing me through that video? Not only will I kick you out from here, I will sue you and you're your friends' asses to hell. Believe me, man. I will fuck the happiness of everyone who knows you. Everyone. You think a stupid video can do something to me? Who will you show it to Saurav? The police. What do you think they will do? You think after you show them the video, it won't leak out. What if it does? What will happen to those very sweet girls, Saurav? Would you like their blood on your hands? Would you destroy their lives? So, what did you think, asshole? You can get through to me with that bloody video? Get this, not only will I eat your jobs, I will make sure that you don't get to anywhere in the entire damned industry.'

Saurav was sweating now. 'I w . . . will . . . will . . . go to the board,' he stammered.

'Aha! Very intelligent. What do you think? They are innocent? I have the security tapes, Saurav. *Everyone* is fucking the shit out in the car park. Oh, am I forgetting something. Your very beloved sir, Deb, is smashing some very expensive car in one of them. I believe it was Sumita's. I am sure she is going to love it! I wonder if he now has that kind of money to pay her back for the damage he did to the car. A criminal case would do loads to his career.'

'What do you want me to do . . .?'

'That is more like it. Here is the deal. Give me the video and sign some affidavit of some obscene amount, some even your father won't be able to pay, that it is the only copy. Once you do that. I may give you your job.'

'And my friends retain their jobs?'

'Oh, no, no, no! Did I not tell you? I am calling the shots here. I can get away with not giving you anything. Remember, you cannot do anything with it.'

He was right. He couldn't. If he tried, he would ruin the lives of two very young women. He could not possibly have done that.

*Remember, you cannot do anything with it*

*Remember, you cannot do anything with it.*

*Remember, you cannot do anything with it.*

Saurav kept repeating these lines in his head which was now heavy with the guilt of costing his friends their jobs.

'Sir . . .' he said.

'Seems like you have decided.'

'I wasn't . . . I wasn't going to give this to the police,' he stuttered.

'Good boy.'

'Or the board.'

'Super. You will keep your job.'

'I always intended to give . . . give it to you,' he said, as he fumbled with words.

'Good for you.'

'Since you are so busy . . .' he said.

'Yes?' Thapar said.

'I was thinking of hand delivering it to your home . . . maybe your wife?'

There was silence.

The trump card, the blind arrow had hit.

There was nothing from the other side.

After a few seconds passed, Thapar said without any hint of worry, 'Go ahead. I don't care. She is okay with all this.'

But it was too late. He was petrified. Thapar never took so long to respond.

Now Saurav was in charge. 'Are you sure? This was what you said. Oh, Anamika you are so good, I can fuck you all day. And my wife, the bitch! I would rather fuck a bitch. And then you laughed, Mr Rajat Thapar.'

'That can't be,' he said. Saurav could tell Thapar was pissing in his pants.

'N96. It might not have the best speakers or alarm. But it has a great microphone.'

'So . . .'

'Time to re-negotiate. I get my job.'

'I don't care,' Rajat said.

'Okay, even I don't. Seems like your kids and your wife are going to love a 40 year old dad who can make twenty year girls scream! I don't give a fuck to your job. Do whatever. But let me tell you, after I show this to your wife, you would be paying more than our combined worth in alimony. You want that, fine with me!'

'Saurav, do you have any idea who you are talking to?'

'Do *you*?'

'What do you want?' Thapar asked finally after he saw that Saurav knew what he was doing. He backed down.

'That is more like it.'

'Hmm . . .'

'My job.'

'Done.'

'And my friends' jobs.'

'Done.'

'Super cool.'

'The video?' he asked meekly.

'Now that I am not signing any affidavit or anything, you won't ever be sure if there exists another copy or not. So, I think you would like to give that a skip.'

'The deal rides on it Saurav.'

'Okay then. The deal is off. None of us was expecting to get our jobs anyway.'

'Fine! It is a deal.'

'And just one question. Is Sumita Bhasin leaving the company?'

'No. Why?'

'I hope you won't miss her, as you would have to throw her out.'

Saurav kept the phone down at that. And opened his laptop.

The recycle bin still had that video.

He clicked on *restore*.

Garima had made him delete it, but he never had the heart of deleting it from the recycle bin. He found the Megha pictures in there too. He deleted them.

It was six when the bell rang that day. Abhi dragged his feet towards the door, his head felt heavy and his body tired.

Till the time he opened the door and saw Shruti standing outside, he didn't really give it a thought as to where he was.

'Shruti?' he asked, puzzled. 'Oh, Shruti, come. Where *were* you?' Abhi asked.

'Out,' Shruti replied. She had thought it would be hard for her to even bear the sight of any one of them, but she was surprisingly happy.

'Look we are very . . . sorry . . .' Abhi said and hugged her.

'It's okay. I should . . .' She hugged him tighter and they both had tears in their eyes.

'We were so worried! Where had you gone? And why did you resign? I mean . . .'

'There was a reason . . . but it is okay! I am not worried.'

'We were. We love you so much. I mean, we are really sorry. We had planned to make . . . '

Shruti saw at this the charts and the tears rolled down.

'This is so sweet . . . This is so sweet!'

'It's nothing . . . I wish we could do something . . .'

'You don't have to . . .' They hugged again.

'I wish things hadn't gone so bad . . .'

'Leave it, Abhi. I want you to meet someone . . .'

At this, Rishab thrust out his hand to shake Abhi's. He had been standing there, witnessing the tearful reunion.

'Rishab,' he said.

'Abhi.'

'Heard a lot about you.'

'I hope it's more good than bad!' Abhi said. 'So? I mean . . . never met you before? College friends?'

'We met yesterday.'

'What?' Abhi asked. 'Where? How?'

'Nothing . . . it is the usual stuff that happens, you know . . . We met, we raced a jet, then we got on that jet, flew to

Delhi, had lunch there and came back,' she said sarcastically.

'Are you drunk?'

'No, I am not. What makes you think I am?'

'If you don't want to tell, it is okay!' Abhi said.

'Abhi, I swear, my tone may not suggest it, but this is the truth,' she said and winked at Rishab.

Rishab smiled.

'Why are you doing this to me?'

'We are doing nothing,' Shruti said. She was still smiling and clutching at Rishab's arm.

'Rishab, what is going on here?'

'She is not lying,' Rishab said.

'You raced a jet. That is what you want me to believe, Rishab?' he asked and stopped. 'Wait . . . this can't be . . . *Rishab?* You look . . . familiar . . .' His eyes were getting wider with each passing second. 'Rishab what?'

'*What* as in?' Shruti asked.

'Surname, damn it?'

'Manchanda,' Rishab said.

'*Rishab Manchanda*?' Abhi asked disbelievingly. '*The* Rishab Manchanda . . .'

'I guess so . . .' he said.

'You guys know each other?' Shruti asked, surprised at Abhi's behaviour.

'I know him . . .'

'How?' Shruti asked.

'The whole country knows him, Shruti! Are you blind? Manchanda Petroleum? Manchanda Textiles? Manchanda Telecom? Are you out of your mind?'

'What? Wait . . . are you? Oh shit! You are . . . are you? Oh no! You are Rishab . . . Manchanda . . . Oh you are . . . You are really?' Shruti kept repeating things like a lunatic.

'Now this is embarrassing.'

'Why didn't you tell me?' Shruti asked.

'You didn't ask.'

'Oh my god! Shit, shit, shit.' She held her head in her hands.

The commotion got the rest three of them up, who were buried in the blankets till then.

'Abhi?' Garima said groggily, eyes still closed, while Saurav and Riya were staring goggle eyed at Rishab. 'I had a strange dream . . . that Shruti was home . . . and Rishab Manchanda . . . you know him, right? That super-hot guy from business world? He is here . . . strange no?'

'Garima, get up,' Abhi said.

'In a while,' she said, as Saurav continued to stare at Rishab. He shifted places in embarrassment. He felt like a zoo animal.

'For a minute please . . .'

'Oh my god! What on earth . . . Is he really him? Are you . . .? What? Why?' She threw the blanket aside and got up on her knees and opened her eyes.

'Yes, he is,' Abhi said.

'Saurav?'

'Yes, Riya?'

'Is this Rishab Manchanda? Really?' Riya asked. She turned to Rishab, 'Are you . . .? Oh shit! I love you so much! I mean, you came on the cover of Business World . . . your suit was fabulous . . .'

'Riya?' Saurav said.

'Yes?'

'Shut up,' he said as he put his hand across her mouth painfully.

They both waved from where they were sitting. They stared and smiled stupidly at Rishab.

After every one had done his or her bit of getting surprised and staring, there were hugs all around. For those few moments, they had forgotten that Shruti had come back. Once they realized that, tears rolled down, apologies were exchanged and God was thanked for everything. Everyone was sorry and every one cried their hearts out.

They told each other how they would always be there for each other and how their lives were incomplete without each other. Garima and Shruti found it hard to keep the flow of tears in check. After a good half hour, things crawled back to normalcy.

'So, what's the story?' Saurav asked.

And then Shruti started to narrate every moment of what happened to three enraptured listeners, who alternated between looking at her and a red faced Rishab.

She skipped the last part of their meeting and left them to guess what must have happened.

'Did it really not strike you?' Abhi asked what Saurav had already asked a million times during Shruti's narration.

'No, it didn't. One more time you ask that, and I will kick you,' Shruti said.

'Okay. And yes, now that the big shock is over, I have something to tell you guys . . .'

'What?' Abhi asked him as all eyes turned to him.

'Thapar called . . .' Saurav said.

Their hearts skipped a beat.

'The video. He knew about it.'

'What? How? I knew something was going to go wrong. I told you Saurav! It was a bad idea. We are screwed,' Garima panicked.

'What did he say?' Abhi asked, as he tried to calm Garima.

'Turns out Rajat is quite a pussy in front of his wife.'

'Come to the point, Saurav,' Garima said irritably.

'The point is, he kind of tried to freak me out, but when I said that I would give it to his wife, he kind of pissed his pants and gave us our jobs and promised he would fire Sumita. That is it, in very short words.'

'*Are you serious?* Abhi asked.

'Do I look like I am laughing?'

'What exactly happened?' Garima asked, still not believing what he said.

'What crap? First you tell me to come to the point. So, I told you. That is what happened! We all have our jobs. Shruti too!'

After that, they all shouted and danced and hugged as Rishab watched on.

'I am so happy for you,' Garima said to Shruti as they both entered the kitchen to make something for the guys.

'Thank you.'

'I am so glad that things are back to what they were like before.'

'Better,' Shruti said.

'Yes, better. It is unbelievable, isn't it? Rishab, probably the smartest, maybe the richest guy in India . . . just when you needed . . .'

'The richest . . .'

'What?'

'Yes, he is the richest. His own personal worth is 6 billion dollars. Add his father's to his, and he is fifth richest in the world. He is the major shareholder in their telecom and textile firms anyway . . . not to mention . . .'

'How do you know so much? I thought . . .'

'I didn't know you would actually believe that I didn't know who he was. I knew who he was the moment I first saw him walk up to me in the nightclub last night,' Shruti said. 'I knew he was Rishab Manchanda. He is my rich guy.'

She looked at Garima and said, 'Now that is luck, isn't it? Life is fair, after all.'

Meanwhile, Saurav and Abhi drove to the nearest market to get something for them.

'It is so cool that we can be together now,' Saurav said.

'I know.'

'You owe me a thank you, man! I know I would have proved to be a major reason had you been kicked out. But still, you weren't!'

'Thanks, man. But it wouldn't have been too bad to lose the job either.'

'What? You were sucking up to this since day one.'

'But now, I have Garima.'

'So?'

'She said I could work with her dad if I wanted to. That would be cool, won't it? Managing a business and stuff.'

'But . . . she does have a brother, right?'

'No. She doesn't! It is all hers.'

'Oh yeah! Shruti is the one who has a brother . . .'

'Hmm . . .'

'Nice.'

'Isn't it?' Abhi smiled. 'My rich girlfriend.'

# Epilogue

And the year passed and Silverman got back to its feet.

Dinesh and Sameer are doing well for themselves.

Shruti left the company and moved to Mumbai with Rishab. They fly down to Hyderabad often.

For lunch, dinner or brunch.

Shruti now has a flying license.

She paid off the debt of his father. They don't talk now no matter how much they call her.

Saurav is still working in Silverman Finance. Riya joined Silverman too. Rajat and Saurav have never talked after that day, except one. Riya was the only person Silverman hired that year.

Saurav sold his car after Rishab gifted him his Porsche. He weighs only eighty now.

Garima and Abhi are still together. They are very much in love. They are moving to Delhi next month. Garima's parents really like Abhi and want him to help them run the business.

Avantika and I are marrying the next year.

And I work more than these people. Really. Six hours a day.

I met these guys last at Shruti's engagement.

It was a glamorous do. Film stars were the order of the day.

Shruti was looking gorgeous in her blazing blue glittery *saree* that Riya chose for her.

I caught her alone for a moment and we hugged. She never looked happier. When you down three glasses of champagne, it does that to you.

'Fairytale, eh? And sure, you look like a princess! Awesome. I have always had the hots . . .'

'Thanks,' she said in a slurred speech.

'No, you are looking ravishing! And isn't this nice? The youngest, richest guy in India falls in love with you when you just lost everything . . . I still find it hard to believe.'

'Love is a strange thing,' she said, a little lost, a little drunk from all the expensive champagne.

'It sure is. How much time has it been? A year? He still loves you as much?'

'It's been two years, not one. Two years since I talked to Sachin . . . don't know . . . . who knows where he is . . .'

'*Rishab*, I meant . . .'

'Him? Oh, him . . . Yes, he loves me. Of course I love him, too . . .' She laughed out and added. ' . . . Till I find someone better.'

We both laughed out. That last line sounded vaguely familiar. The smile faded away quite quickly from her face as she gulped her drink and looked me.

'Love can wait . . .' she said and looked at me before finally smiling at me and added, 'It's all about money, honey!'

She walked away, looking at her ten million diamond ring.